Caro... of man and baby in the apartment window

She stared at the image for the longest time, finding it difficult to tear herself away from the touching scene—or from the evidence of Rick's duplicity.

So much for faith! Even though she'd pleaded for the truth about the missing heir, for an answer he'd remained silent.

Still, the sight of the pair tugged at her heart. Even after ten years, Rick held his magic over her. She watched his head move in animation, no doubt conversing with the child. A lullaby perhaps? A fairy tale?

But the baby's future wasn't his decision to make. No wonder Rick hadn't wanted her to investigate his personal life. He had all the evidence to seal the case. The answer to the riddle.

All twenty-five pounds worth!

Dear Reader,

What is more appealing, more enduring than *Cinderella, Beauty and the Beast* and *Pygmalion*? Fairy tales and legends are basic human stories, retold in every age, in their own way. Romance stories, at their heart, are the happily ever after of every story we listened to as children.

That was the inspiration for our 1993 yearlong Lovers & Legends miniseries. Each month, one book is a fairy tale retold in sizzling Temptation-style!

This month we have *Rumpelstiltskin,* another favorite tale wherein the heroine is the main protagonist. She is faced with solving the riddle of the billion-dollar baby—at stake is her future, both professionally and emotionally.

In the coming months we have stories from bestselling authors Kelly Street, *The Virgin and the Unicorn* (unicorn myths), Gina Wilkins, *When It's Right* (*The Princess and the Pea*), Lynn Michaels, *Second Sight* (*The Ugly Duckling*) and JoAnn Ross, *The Prince and the Showgirl* (*Cinderella*).

We hope you enjoy the magic of Lovers & Legends, plus all the other terrific Temptation novels coming in 1993! Don't miss #436, *Moonstruck Lovers* by JoAnn Ross, a love story truly out of this world and #448 *Love Slave* by Mallory Rush—the pages are practically combustible!

Enjoy the magic of romance.

Birgit Davis-Todd
Senior Editor

P.S. We love to hear from our readers.

The Missing Heir

Leandra Logan

Harlequin Books

TORONTO • NEW YORK • LONDON
AMSTERDAM • PARIS • SYDNEY • HAMBURG
STOCKHOLM • ATHENS • TOKYO • MILAN
MADRID • WARSAW • BUDAPEST • AUCKLAND

For my mother, Delores Leonard
An extraordinary grandma, golfer and gambler—
plus a whole lot more!

Published March 1993

ISBN 0-373-25533-0

THE MISSING HEIR

1

THE TELEPHONE'S RING pierced the dark silent bedroom, rousing Caron Carlisle from a deep sleep. She inched a long slender arm out from under the bedding, patting the nightstand in the search of her white trimline. It sounded off a bleating baker's dozen before she managed to draw the receiver down into her cocoon of covers and greet her caller with a husky hello.

"Good morning!"

For milkmen and vampires maybe. Caron groaned softly as she peeked over the hem of her sheet into the predawn darkness.

"Hello, hello, is anybody home?" a hearty male voice demanded.

Not recognizing the caller, Caron poised a trigger-happy thumb over the disconnect button. "Do we . . ."

"Well, we used to."

She slanted a brow warily. "When?"

"Ah, seems like yesterday."

Caron failed to swallow back a huge yawn. "I believe you have the wrong party."

"I'm looking for the Caron Carlisle who works for the law firm of snap, crackle, pop."

"Sharp, Krandell and Peterson," she croaked in correction, inching her shoulders up onto her pillows. This night owl nut had the right number after all. Her unlisted number.

"Ah, Caron. I've found you, then."

The unknown caller's deep timbre sent a delicious tingle through her languid limbs. His voice held a familiar edge, as did his easy manner—a manner that somehow made arrogance an attribute. Caron rubbed her forehead in a foggy jumble. Who was this sweet-talkin' bozo?

"I hope you don't mind my calling at this hour," he continued conversationally. "I just couldn't wait another minute. In my line of work I often keep odd hours. Figured you do to."

"As a matter of fact, I don't," Caron differed cautiously, struggling in vain to place the man. As an associate of one of Denver's most prestigious law offices, it paid to be discreet. He could just be a client. Though most were on the stuffy side, a few live ones slipped in on occasion! And somehow, all the . . . unusual . . . cases ended up on her desk.

"Perry Mason puts you to shame, Caron. He's available at all hours of the day and night."

"Della Street was the available one," she automatically replied, a fan of the show herself. "The loyal secretary who forwarded only urgent calls to his *unlisted number.*"

"He's the only lawyer I've ever trusted, too," the calm male voice contended, not revealing how he had managed to get through to her. "Until now. Until this morning."

Morning? Caron sincerely doubted it. She grabbed the clock radio off the nightstand, drawing it up to her nearsighted eyes. The red letters glowed 4:49. "Do you realize it's still nighttime to most of America?"

He heaved a depreciative sigh. "Still argue each and every point, I see."

"You can't *see* a thing on my end."

"*See* what I mean?"

Caron's heart stopped in her chest. Could it be *him?* No. Not after all these years. But he did like the "Perry Mason" show, even back then.... She cleared her throat, her mouth forming an O as she summoned the voice lost somewhere in her cottony throat. "Who? Who are you?"

"Well, I was hoping to soften you up a little first," he confessed with obvious amusement. "This is Rick Wyatt, Caron. From the class of '83. Truman High School."

"Hotshot!" Caron bolted upright to a seated position, the clock plopping into her lap.

A deep chuckle rippled across the line. "Yeah, Hotshot it is. Don't hang up on me now."

Hanging would be too good for him! Or was it just right? She toyed with the phone line, pinching several inches of it into a small noose. She squeezed it so hard that her fingers soon throbbed purple. It was no surprise that she still had some leftover emotion for this smooth-talking class rebel, this intelligent egomaniac who had taken fiendish pleasure in driving her to distraction at every turn. But the intensity of those feelings was indeed shocking to this savvy twenty-eight-year-old attorney who thought she knew herself inside out!

This run-in might be totally unexpected, but it was not beyond her control, she decided, straightening the wire with a determined jerk. Childhood neighbors, she and Hotshot had a history of niggling at each other's weak spots. Their relationship had heated up to explosive levels during their senior year when Rick had invaded her turf in the structured high school arena, taking his snappy show off the streets and into the student council chambers. Rick hadn't cared a whit about bettering the school. Toying with its policies from the revered president's chair had been nothing more than a game of skill to him. A chance to buck the system with a rally of loyal students in his wake.

Caron had eyed that president's seat with the longing of a dedicated student. After three years on the council, building up her support, she'd been defeated. President Hotshot went on to charm everyone. As vice president she found her more conservative policies were overruled over and over again.

But that was a long time ago, she reminded herself. They'd been out of touch for ten years, since graduation. He could no longer draw her into an emotional tizzy with a few words. Rick's attempt to bait her into a flare-up before even identifying himself, however, was vintage Hotshot behavior. Her rising to that bait was par for the well-traveled course of yesterday, too.

"Still up to your old tricks, I see," she eventually tossed back with forced smoothness. "Calling me now, knowing full well I'd still be in bed."

"Sorry about the hour. Please believe that I'd never stoop so low as to tease a woman in her most intimate spot. Not without permission anyway."

Caron held the receiver at arm's length for a moment so he wouldn't hear her quaking breath. His voice was still a masculine purr—French silk pie smooth. Caron was obsessed with sweets. Somewhere back in time, Rick's chocolate syrup eyes, full of mischief, mayhem and seductiveness, had been an irresistible treat to her. Instead she said sternly, "Does this nocturnal nonsense have a purpose?"

"All my moves have a purpose now. Though I still like to seize the moment, make it sizzle—"

"Well, don't expect me to hop into the frying pan with you!"

"I'm unavoidable when I want to be."

When he wanted to be. Rick Wyatt had dodged her for a decade. She focused on this hard nugget of truth as her insides began to cook, as if she were truly flat on her back in that pan.... "No need to explain your tactics to me. They're still legendary in my mind."

"There isn't time now for fond reminiscences, Caron. I'm calling about the baby."

Beds and babies. Dreaminess enveloped her groggy senses. Back in school, many a girl's fantasy had centered on Rick Wyatt and those very two things. Caron herself had often wondered what their child would look like, if it would have her thick chestnut hair and Rick's handsome features. "What are you talking about?" she managed to ask softly.

"The billon-dollar baby, of course! At least that's what you people are calling him."

His reply yanked her back to reality with a sharp, leashlike tug. "How do you know about the baby search? That's a confidential matter being handled by snap, crackle, pop!"

His chuckle crispened. "You haven't seen the morning headlines yet."

"Certainly not while asleep!" Energized with panic and fury she reached over to snap on the bedside lamp and grab her glasses, jamming them haphazardly on the bridge of her perfectly sloped nose. She blinked behind the lenses, primed for action. Then froze for a long aggravating moment, finding it difficult to acknowledge the embarrassingly obvious even to herself.

"Rick?"

"Yeah?"

"My copy of the *Denver Press* isn't due for an hour."

"Billion-Dollar Grandchild Sought By Douglas Ramsey," Rick dutifully recited for the paperless.

"Oh, no!" Caron reeled back, banging her head against the maple headboard. With effort she bit off a yelp as pain shot through her skull.

"You still there, Quick Draw? You okay?"

"Yes and yes!"

"So, you in on the case?"

"Most definitely." She massaged the bruise on her scalp through a tangle of mussed brown hair, wincing in pain over the new bump and her old nickname. The student body had tagged her Quick Draw because of her talent for sharp uptakes in class. Then and now the name sounded downright affectionate coming from Rick's mouth. How dare he, after dumping her so unceremoniously years ago?

"So give me the lowdown, Caron. What's this Ramsey guy's angle?"

Caron gripped the phone in a tight fist. This couldn't be happening to her all over again—Rick Wyatt entering her life in this upstaging way, on her most important case! It was even more humiliating to admit ignorance to this man. But what choice did she have?

"Rick, I don't know anything about the newspaper article."

"Hmm . . . You sure you have the skinny on this baby search?"

"I most certainly do! I'm in charge of it!"

"Really? You losing your Quick Draw touch or what?"

Fury boiled her blood at his challenge. She didn't like being caught by him this way: in bed and in the dark. "Maybe you could fill me in on the story," she requested with deliberate calmness.

"Glad to help you out," he merrily obliged with a rustle of paper. "It explains how Douglas Ramsey, founder of the Ramsey Department Store chain is searching for his alleged grandson. Alleged. That means he's not sure the kid exists, right?"

"Yes. In short, it means that we have no proof as of yet, that there is a grandson."

"Then it goes on, blah, blah, blah—"

"Fill in the blah blahs," Caron anxiously broke in, shoving her glasses farther up her nose.

"Oh. Well, it just gives some background on Ramsey, explaining how he has been estranged from his son, James, for much of the boy's life. That James died of cancer last year." There was a slight pause on the line. "You know about this stuff already, of course."

"Of course," Caron agreed, her brain ticking madly over the turn of events. Douglas Ramsey would be livid when he found out about this invasion of privacy. What if he blamed her? Trying to quell the trepidation mounting with every beat of her heart, she probed further. "I imagine it reports how James Ramsey spoke of a baby son before he passed away. That the elder man is desperately searching for his second-generation heir."

"Yep. According to the article, not only is the alleged grandson entitled to the Ramsey estate when he comes of age, but there is a finder's fee of a million at stake."

Caron gasped in shock. "*Douglas Ramsey* is offering a million dollars for information leading to the baby?"

"Right on."

"Then he's behind the article himself?" She knew her voice was a squeal of utter amazement, but she couldn't help it. The billionaire had obviously taken the reins of the baby search right out of her hands. It was downright irritating that he hadn't discussed this showy move with her. But it was totally unforgivable that he hadn't at least warned her as late as last night, giving her ammo to de-fuse Rick's guessing game. Oh, how satisfying that would've been.

"Maybe you better get together with this rich old guy and compare notes," Rick suggested.

"This is going to attract every baby bounty hunter in the state of Colorado!"

"Baby bounty hunter," he repeated slowly. "Say it fast three times, Quick Draw!" he urged excitedly. "Let's see if you've still got that rapid-fire delivery."

"I've still got it."

"Just testing the sharpness of your wit," he explained good-humoredly. "I have to be certain you're still as reliable as you were in school."

Such praise coming from a colleague at work would have delighted her to no end. Coming from the incorrigible Hotshot, it opened an unhealed wound deep within her heart where a shy, plump teenager still dwelled.

"You seem sort of dazed by all of this, Caron."

His observation was undeniably true. She was trying to digest the fact that Douglas Ramsey, the big man himself, had betrayed her big-time. After the great pains her law firm had taken to keep this baby search out of the limelight, he'd gone public on his own. She'd advised the billionaire against this tactic from the start, claiming people would go crazy if they thought they had a chance of plugging into the Ramsey empire by producing a baby boy heir.

And she had believed Douglas Ramsey had implicit faith in her judgment! Respect for her as a person. The elderly man had actually taken a fatherly interest in her, beyond attorney-client boundaries. Sure, he was an old grump accustomed to getting his own way. Sure, he was bossy to a fault. Perhaps he was incapable of trusting anyone completely. She certainly wouldn't trust *him* from now on!

"The paper says any inquiries concerning the baby should be made to your law firm," Rick went on to report amid the rustle of paper.

"Well, thank goodness the old goat did that much!"

"So, he is as difficult as they say," Rick deduced with a hint of triumph.

"Yes! No!" She stumbled for a fair assessment. "So, what's it to you anyhow, Rick?"

"I wish to inquire, of course."

Caron's brow furrowed in suspicion. "Is this one of your tricks?"

"No, Caron, honestly it isn't," he assured, sounding a bit hurt over the accusation. "If you still do your homework as diligently as you used to, you know that James lived here in the old neighborhood for the past few years."

Caron's brain began to tick faster. Of course James had, not far from her parents' old place. Dare she ask Rick flat out? Obviously he still took great pleasure toying with her sensible side. She took a deep breath and asked, "Do you know the whereabouts of Douglas Ramsey's grandson, Rick?"

"What if I do?"

"Then you should be in my office today, that's what!"

"I'm calling you at home because I must insist upon anonymity. Caron, you are just the reliable go-between I need."

That word again. *Reliable.* Yuck! "A go-between isn't needed in a case like this. No one has broken the law. No one is in danger."

"You'd just be doing your job," he pointed out. "Under the covers so to speak."

"I like to play it by the book, Rick."

"Still the same philosophical, rule-hugging girl of yesterday," he judged in heaving disappointment.

"Still the class rebel intent on making his own rules," she tossed back. "Bound and determined to rub me the wrong way while doing it."

"Our last duel was sure a doozy," he recalled with suspect fondness. "Over that punch spill on your prom dress, remember?"

Caron found herself magically transported back to the humiliating moment a decade behind them. "I believe I called you a girl-mooching egomaniac who couldn't handle a punch."

"Quick to the draw," he concurred. "You know, it's kind of funny now."

"Is it?"

"Yeah. I operate a Laundromat and could remove that infamous stain in no time. My place is called Hotshots. You know, because of the shots of water in the washers, the air in the dryers. And of course my nickname."

Caron already knew of his business venture, located a block off Fairfax Avenue near Truman High School. Apparently it was currently a neighborhood hangout as well as a place to clean clothes. She had no firsthand knowledge of the place, for she hadn't been back to those old stomping grounds in a long time. Not since her parents had moved to a trendy Denver suburb.

"Hey, I bet you don't want to help me because you're still stinging over old wounds," he chided.

His perception rankled her. "I have no time to bear grudges over fizzled romance and lost student council issues. I'm busy trying cases and saving people's butts."

"Then have mercy on one very special talcum-powdered butt, for old times' sake."

"Your butt or the baby's?"

"Cute, Quick Draw, real cute."

"Seriously, Rick, I'm doing everything I can to help this child attain his legacy."

"Maybe that favor isn't quite as simple as it seems. What if there are extenuating circumstances?"

"Such as?"

"Who's to say that the baby might not be better off in his current situation? You said yourself that Ramsey's a goat."

"But—"

"And money isn't everything, you know," he forged on. "I've got the feeling that if Ramsey finds this boy, he won't be willing to let go of him even if the setup doesn't suit the kid. If Ramsey is a genuine blackheart trying to control the whole show, the child could end up in a miserable existence."

"I would tell any prospective representative of the heir to keep in mind that the infant may never be affected by Douglas Ramsey himself. Considering his age . . ."

"The guy is only seventy-seven. He's still at the helm of his department store chain. He could be around for aeons."

"You really should step forward," she advised, trying to conceal her eagerness. "We'll start by putting together an affidavit."

"Can't you talk with me friend to friend?"

"We must go through the proper channels here, Rick."

"I get it. Law-and-order Quick Draw trying to keep the streets free of rebels like me. Just as you tried in the school council."

"I did not! I, ah, just thought I deserved to be in charge."

"Well, I still don't run by the stuffy rules of the world."

Caron huffed impatiently into the receiver. "Like it or not, this case is business. Billion-dollar big business. It would be much better handled in the office and out of the bedroom. At a decent hour!"

"I'm calling you to avoid all that!" Rather reluctantly, he added, "I hoped for a personal touch, Caron. You did so many little favors for me when we were young. It seems natural, us sitting down to iron out this heir's dilemma. There just happens to be a new Chinese place just down the street from here...."

He was trying to remove her from her work setting. Wrap her around his... She gave her head a clearing-house shake. "Rick, sitting in my office for a little chat is not going to turn you into a conservative toad. Let me pencil you in for nine today—"

"Put your damn pencil away!" he growled in defeat. "I only tangle with empty white collars. I clean 'em up and send 'em back."

"You still can't be bucking the system every inch of the way!" Caron cried in wonder.

"Whatever happened to us, Quick Draw?"

"A question I've asked myself many times," she admitted, matching his bewilderment.

"Look, this idea was a mistake," he said in a more tempered tone. "Never mind."

"But Rick—"

"Forget I called, Caron. If you care a whit about our history, neighborhood loyalty, whatever, you won't tell any of your white collars about me."

Before Caron could respond, the dial tone buzzed in her ear. She slammed down the telephone, slammed down the clock and was looking for something more to slam when her overhead light flicked on, brightly illuminating her mauve and gray bedroom. Caron squinted up to find Megan Gage, her lifelong friend and current roommate, standing in the doorway with her hand on the wall switch.

"What are you going on about?" Megan entered with a weary yet curious expression on her round, dimpled face. Just home from the night shift at Mercy Hospital, the petite blonde was wearing a crisp white nurse's uniform and identification badge. "Wrestling with a bad dream? The clock? The radio?"

"All of the above!" Caron swung her long slender legs over the side of the bed. "Men are the most maddening creatures!"

"You been wrestling with one of those, too?" Instant interest sparked her features. "I thought I heard you on the telephone when I walked in."

Caron hopped to her feet, peeling off her orange nightshirt as she charged the dresser for panties and bra. "I just got word that the billion-dollar baby deal has made the newspapers." Caron tugged on her underthings, then moved to the chair where last night's lavender jogging suit sat in a heap. "You know what this means, don't you?" she wailed. "I've lost control of the hunt for the missing heir. My precious chance to make a real mark at the firm! Oh, snap, crackle and pop will be livid."

"I've never heard you refer to Sharp, Krandell and Peterson that way before," Megan balked. "But I like it."

Caron winced in disgust. Rick's glib attitude was already affecting her!

"So, who is the madman who called about the news leak? Douglas Ramsey?"

Caron struggled with her sweatshirt, her head eventually popping through the crew neck. "Douglas Ramsey is the blasted leak. Spilled his guts without a word to me."

"So, who called?" Megan pressed. Always interested in her best friend's cases, she found this story of wealth, secret romance and potential heirs especially intriguing.

"Who has you slamming things around and snapping like a wildcat?"

Caron sat down on the edge of the mattress to slip into her athletic shoes, deliberately drawing out the moment. She eventually peeked up from her laces with glinting green eyes full of passion and fury. "Hotshot."

Megan hooted in disbelief. "Get serious! That old high school tease line isn't amusing anymore. The days of our wishing for that magical call are long over."

"I mean it, Meg." Caron stood up, towering over her friend. "Who else could put me in fits without laying a hand on me?"

"Your mother for one," Megan promptly specified.

"Well, Rick Wyatt takes the prize this morning. Catches me in bed. Off guard. Uninformed. Leaves me feeling like an utter fool as he goes on to fill me in about my own case."

"So, Rick has an interest in the billionaire baby. Wonder if he knows that most of the girls in the class of '83 would consider a baby of his to be worth a billion?"

Caron snatched a brush from the dresser and gingerly styled her hair around the bruise on the back of her head. "With that monster ego of his? I'm sure he knows."

Megan rubbed her palms together with glee. "So, how'd he sound?"

"Like a cross between James Dean and Dracula."

"A rebel without a neck to bite?"

"A rebel without a Timex!" Caron dropped the brush with a clatter. "The jerk apparently keeps vampire hours at that Laundromat of his and gets the paper fresh off the press."

"Still cocky, eh?"

Caron rolled her eyes. "I'll say. Though there was something new running beneath his rebel savvy. A thread of vulnerability. As if this baby thing has gotten to him somehow."

Megan nodded. "Must've taken a lot of guts to call here, considering the storms you two have ridden together. He must have one heck of a lead."

"Let's hope not. He blew up when I tried to get him into the office. Insisted I forget about his call. My entire career hinges on tracking this heir and he ordered me to secrecy concerning his potential part in it."

"Just think, your firm's spent a small fortune beating the bushes for this baby, and Rick Wyatt, the hotshot hunk of our old neighborhood, may hold the key to it all."

Caron glared into space. "You know I could never stand for Rick to know more about a subject than I did in school. Now he's back, with the jump on me all over again. Will I ever get the best of that man?"

Megan fluttered her pale lashes. "Intriguing challenge."

"And then there's that crafty bear, Douglas Ramsey," Caron sputtered. "He's gone behind my back and offered a million-dollar reward for information leading to his grandson."

Megan's small frame teetered with the weight of the news. "Wow! That reward include you?"

Caron flashed her a look of loving exasperation. "No, Meggy, I'm just the hired help."

"Oh, shucks. I could see us in new threads, on a Club Med vacation." She thought hard, then brightened with a brainstorm. "Say, if Rick gets the dough, maybe he'll take us on a sweet little trip."

Caron snorted. "We've been out of touch for ten years. And the old baggage is there. He still wants to bend all the rules, and you know it's not my nature to bend."

"He's one to break a rule or two for," Megan recommended playfully, clutching her heart just below her nameplate. "I'll bet he's still gorgeous."

"A person can lose his looks without losing his nerve," Caron pointed out with a wicked curl to her mouth.

"A mere decade has passed."

"Appearances can change. Take me, for example," Caron invited without coquettishness.

"You're the siren you always aspired to be," Megan acknowledged, surveying Caron's coltish figure, tinted chestnut hair bobbed at the chin, and resculptured nose. "But I have a feeling Rick's still high octane."

"Probably," Caron grumpily relented. "But it's a fuel that doesn't burn me up anymore."

"I wonder if a girl can outgrow that kind of burn."

The pair shared a brief telepathic moment, honed to sharp clarity by their years of friendship. Inseparable since the sixth grade, they'd shared every secret, every dream with each other. It had been their ambition to earn their respective degrees, buy a town house, and live together as sisters until the right men came along—which is exactly what they were doing.

Potential husband material had moved in and out of their master plan with the passage of time, no one quite right to have and to hold forever. Caron found it heartbreakingly frustrating that she always ended up comparing her men to Rick. His delicious blend of street sense and good humor had delighted and tormented her through most of her girlhood. The memories grew more poignant with the passage of time. Most of them, anyway...

"Maybe you better send one of your fellow associates over to interview him," Megan suggested, her creamy brow furrowed in concern.

Caron released a ponderous sigh. "I don't think I can do that to him, even if he deserves it."

"This thing between you two is so emotion-packed," Megan murmured doubtfully. "So much about prom night remains unsettled. And you know it's churned and churned within you all these years."

"He already brought up our little tussle himself," Caron reported with a cringe, recalling her own retaliatory measures of the night. After Rick spilled the punch on her, she'd stuffed a sandwich into his scarlet cummerbund, popping a button on his white ruffled shirt as she'd grabbed a handful of fabric. The class would never forget that scene. Especially their poor respective dates. The abandoned pair had marched off in embarrassment and anger.

"Maybe I'll have a stroke of luck and someone will come in the office with a good solid lead in the right direction," she declared hopefully, "leaving Rick completely out of it."

"Yeah, then you could just forget all about his call," Megan proposed, a little heavy on the solicitude.

Caron flashed her a shrewd look. "Why, then I'd have to forget about our little wager, Meg."

Megan stared into Caron's dancing eyes and emitted a shriek. "You don't intend to cash in on that bet after all this time!"

"I sure do," Caron announced magnanimously, abruptly leaving the room.

"There must be a statute of limitations on bets made twelve years ago by a couple of dreamy teenyboppers," Megan cried in mortification, trailing after Caron as she roamed the town house.

"You'd make me do it in a shot," Caron maintained, pausing at the kitchen counter to zip her purse shut.

"Of course I would," Megan agreed without shame. "But you're the humanitarian of the house. The one who became a lawyer to make the world a more just place to live."

Caron moved to the short staircase leading to the entryway, jingling her car keys. "On that cheery note, I'm off to buy my newspapers, to see if I can make this world a better place for one billionaire baby. If you'd like to go over our agreement," she added in afterthought, "it's still pressed between the pages of my '81 yearbook. Where it's been since the day we signed it."

"We're talkin' ancient history!" Megan howled, throwing her arms in the air as she ran for the shelves.

Caron clucked in suspect sympathy. "You'll see that we set no time limit, Meg. The first of us to get a call from Hotshot—whether it be about a homework assignment, a sock hop, or the temperature outside—is the true and real winner. You have to pay up."

Megan thumbed through the yearbooks in search of the right annual. "I could get arrested!"

"Not to worry. This humanitarian will represent you *pro bono*."

Something hit the door seconds later as Caron crossed the lawn to the driveway. Most likely *The Truman High School Memorandum, 1981*.

2

"'BILLIONAIRE BABY AT LARGE!'" Douglas Ramsey proudly read the headline of the *Denver Daily* before folding it in two and slapping it down on the conference table at Sharp, Krandell and Peterson.

Ensconced in one of the firm's large glass-walled offices with the billionaire and two of the partners, Caron noted that Ramsey, in his late seventies, was still an imposing figure. His gray flannel suit cut a smooth swath from his broad shoulders, his coarse hair properly covered his balding head and his blue eyes glittered hard with authority behind their bifocal barrier. He was a man to be reckoned with, one who often sought to maintain the upper hand by sheer intimidation.

Caron also realized that Ramsey was now searching their faces for shock value, for some dismay over his stunt. But of course it was too late. Hotshot had upstaged the unassuming billionaire with his early morning phone call. Caron had in turn immediately called her superiors after purchasing an armload of papers featuring the bad news. They had held a powwow before office hours to rethink their strategy. Ramsey had certainly muffed their plans to tread softly.

As Caron predicted, the partners were outraged. Up to this point, they'd been humoring the rich old client as little more than a courtesy, far more focused on the legal workings of the Ramsey Department Store chain. They considered the baby hunt a silly waste of time, called it

Ramsey's Folly behind his back. It had been judged a job worthy of an associate only, and ultimately hoisted into Caron's lap. A lap that ironically had never held a real live baby. Caron had been considered the perfect underling for the job, not because of her skills as an attorney, but because Douglas Ramsey had taken such a shine to her during her two-year tenure at the firm. The strategy had been for Caron to put some steam into the search, just enough to satisfy Ramsey and his ninety-year-old spinster sister, Agatha. It was theorized that the baby most likely didn't exist and the search would die out. Naturally Caron resented this attitude and fervently hoped to find the baby heir, prove her worth to the company once and for all.

Unfortunately her month-long investigation had turned up precious little. There were no records, no gossipy biddies at James's former apartment building prepared to gleefully spill all. The entire riddle was based upon a deathbed statement James supposedly made to his Aunt Agatha. It was the general consensus of the partners that the ninety-year-old merely had fallen asleep at her nephew's bedside and dreamt the whole thing.

Of course there was no turning back now, not on the crest of Ramsey's publicity stunt. Not with the entire world on alert, waiting for the law firm of Sharp, Krandell and Peterson to come up with one billion-dollar baby. The lawyers all knew it was Douglas Ramsey's intention to get them searching more diligently. It had worked! Caron had to fight hard at the meeting to keep control of the case. In the end, the partners had conceded to her wishes.

"Yes," Ramsey crowed on in pride. "This is how you get action, fellows. And, miss," he added, shifting in his seat to glance warmly at his favorite associate, standing nearby in a flattering cream-colored gabardine suit and forest green blouse.

Two of the firm's partners, William Peterson and Lester Sharp, regarded Caron from their seats as well, expecting her to pick up the ball she'd fought so hard to keep in her court only one short hour ago. She had contended that no one in the firm knew better how to handle Douglas Ramsey than she. The claim went unchallenged. For the time being.

Caron figured his devotion to her stemmed from many small seeds. The complicated legal work she performed regularly for him. Her open expression of sympathy over the loss of his son. Her instant rapport with his elderly sister. The simple biological fact that she was a woman and would better understand his needs as a grandparent.

Ironically his assumptions concerning her motherly instinct were unfounded. An only child who had preferred to study while her peers baby-sat, she knew nothing about babies. Caring for anyone below the age of reason frightened her more than facing a potentially dangerous client behind prison walls. Having her own family was a far-off dream. At present she concentrated on nothing beyond the career she was carving out as the only female associate of the firm.

It was with her legal prowess that she hoped to impress the billionaire—and achieve her fondest wish, the partnership. True, they mixed business with pleasure on occasion, partaking in everything from hot-air ballooning to roaming the hills of Golden, Ramsey's hometown. He was lonely and confused, searching not only for his grandson, but for his roots, reexamining the early days when things were simple. The department store magnate was quite vigorous for his age and, despite his business dealings, always seemed to have time for Caron and a new excursion. Caron gave him as much attention as her busy day allowed, but was sometimes forced to decline his offers. He didn't like it.

Being forever the manipulator, he frequently tried to lure her away from the firm with job offers in his company. Caron consistently declined, not sure she could tolerate his blustery ways on a day-to-day basis, and not sure she could give up the drama of the courtroom. She'd worked so hard for the chance to stand center stage and sway people with articulate oration. The heavier her court schedule, the happier she was.

"Mr. Ramsey," she began, pacing round the room, "I thought we agreed this investigation would be left to our discretion."

"But you people were getting nowhere, Caron," he grumbled, his bushy gray brows slanting to the bridge of his blunt nose.

"Subtlety takes time."

"I expect this stuffy firm to be miffed by my bawdy offer. But some incentive was needed to beef up this search. Money is something everyone understands. They'll come to us now, rather than vice versa." He held up a large, halting palm as she opened her mouth. "I know you are going to remind me of the security angle. But I don't think babies will be snatched from their cribs and delivered to my doorstep. Without proof positive, I'd never accept a boy as my grandson."

"The huge reward is likely to bring out some enterprising charlatans though," Caron predicted in concern. "We're already getting outrageous calls."

"It won't be so bad, Caron. I whittled down the candidates by asking for a certain heirloom." Ramsey proudly gestured at the newspaper with the largest photograph of himself.

"Just what is this heirloom?" Lester Sharp demanded, twirling a pen in his hands.

"All you need to know is that it's a medal," Ramsey replied with a wily look. "To keep everybody honest, I'm going to keep the precise details to myself for now."

"Bah!" Sharp complained with a gesture of impatience.

"Root through the heap, Lester, and you may just find a nugget of information," Ramsey proclaimed. "A million-dollar nugget that would be worth a billion to a lucky little boy. You single out the prospects with a medal, and I'll speak with them. Here, by appointment. Easy enough."

"We were doing it the easy way, Douglas," William Peterson broke in huffily.

"Four weeks should have been ample time," Ramsey lectured sternly.

"James was a prosperous businessman in his own right," Caron pointed out, "with three print shops across the state. The list of his connections and acquaintances has proven endless."

"A good surgeon slices open his patient, makes the repairs, then sews him back up before the anesthetic wears off, before the patient bleeds to death. It's all in the timing," Ramsey bellowed, slicing the air with his hand. "A quick cut, then in and out."

Caron wandered over to the skyscraper window facing Lincoln Avenue, folding her arms across her chest with a pensive sigh. The removal of Ramsey's kidney last year was obviously still on his metaphoric mind. The perilous surgery followed by his son's death had forced Ramsey to confront mortality in spades. That was the reason for the search for the last Ramsey descendant.

Though impressed with Ramsey's quest to track down his heir, Caron had come to recognize his gruffness, his

uncompromising nature, his reluctance to delegate duties.
Why, his announcement to the papers was a prime example. He was determined to run everything, compulsively bullying employees and family members to the
limit.

It was this very weakness that had gotten him into this
jam in the first place. He'd suffered tremendously over the
years because of his drive and forcefulness. His wife had
passed away some time ago, long after their bitter divorce. His son, James, had sided with his mother, leaving
father and son estranged right up until James's death. The
notion that there might be another Ramsey floating
around in the world was killing the old man.

More than once, however, she'd wondered what he'd do
when he found his grandson. Things that were cut and
dried in Ramsey's mind might not be so in reality. The
child had a mother. Seemingly a mere detail to him. Perhaps the mother knew the score and she and her son were
in hiding. Hiding from the glare of the public Ramsey lifestyle, the beady-eyed glare behind Douglas Ramsey's thick
glasses. Did Caron have the right to yank them into the
limelight? She found herself in a moral quandary over the
possibilities. She found her trust in him wavering more
today than it ever had during their two-year relationship.

And not because of Hotshot's soapbox lecture! Her own
social conscience functioned quite well. Even though she
followed the rules, it didn't mean she didn't question their
value on occasion.

Peterson cleared his throat from his place at the long table, his small dark eyes telling her to soothe the savage
beast. Poised to speak, she paused in uncertainty. This
would be the precise moment to bring up Rick Wyatt and
his claim, show she was on top of the leads flowing in. If
she wanted to be a ruthless player who sought only re-

sults, she could give a full report and perhaps solve the mystery immediately. At worst they'd hit a blind alley. But could she betray a man she'd known since childhood? Despite their clashes, there was still the good stuff. Some of it had been really good stuff. Leave it to him to put her in a compromising position without getting physical!

With all eyes expectantly upon her, Caron took a seat at the table. "Mr. Ramsey," she began awkwardly, "I sincerely wish you hadn't taken matters into your own hands, but since you have . . . Since you have," she repeated in a stronger voice, making the gut decision to give Rick a temporary reprieve, "we have no choice than to adjust, to focus on the prospects who come to us."

"You believe he exists, don't you?" he quizzed sharply.

"I most certainly do," Caron immediately assured so the partners wouldn't have to muster up false support.

"If only Agatha could give us more to go on," he said in regret.

"I've spoken to your sister a few times, sir, and her stories shift with the breeze." Caron tapped a round polished nail on the fat manila folder before her on the table. "I have scads of material here dating back to your childhood."

"Agatha's a dotty rambler," Ramsey rumbled in despair. "No doubt we could be blackmailed a hundred times over with the stuff you've compiled."

"Perhaps a good glitzy book of fiction could be gleaned." Caron's lilting laughter brought a glimmer to Ramsey's ruddy, glum features. "As I say," she went on with a note of levity, "there is too much embellishment for any real chronicle. We need hard facts."

"I know it's difficult to take Agatha's word alone on this," Ramsey conceded. "But that's all we've had all along—her insistence that James claimed to have fathered a baby boy. It's possible that she's just wishing. With her spinsterhood and my aloneness, perhaps it's a diversion to buffer the Ramsey pain. But I can't rest until I know for sure. And every fiber of my being tells me the baby's out there somewhere."

"Agatha is still often as sharp as a tack," Caron encouraged, giving his arm a pat. "She may have gotten the message just right."

"She took James's death hard," he confided, his voice quavering. "His lung cancer was a painful thing for both of us. Outliving one's descendant is a cruel twist of fate. Even near the end, when he agreed to see me, he was distant. And certainly said nothing about a baby. Probably was afraid I'd try to run the child's life as I did his." He drew his forearms on the table and hunched over briefly for a steadying breath.

"The first task is to find the child," Caron consoled. "Meet with the mother, see where all the pieces fit." To her annoyance, Ramsey's face clouded at the mere mention of the mother, just as it always did. Which was why she was giving Hotshot the benefit of the doubt for now. Maybe he was playing the role of the noble protector.

"That should settle things for now," he said in brusque farewell. "I'll forward all inquiries made at the house to your office." Straightening up, he beckoned to his chauffeur seated in the waiting area beyond the glass wall. The distinguished silver-haired man immediately entered the conference room to help the burly billionaire from his chair and into his coat. Everyone else stood up as well, forming a loose semicircle around him.

"By the way, Caron, are you free this Saturday night?" Ramsey asked. "I'm having a little party at my place here in Denver."

A smile twitched at her lips. A little party? It was a huge gala event for the social elite of the state!

"I'm certain she's free," Lester Sharp smoothly intervened.

"You privy to her social calendar?" Ramsey barked with his trademark glare.

"Why, no, of course not," Lester backtracked with a tight-lipped look.

"This is purely a personal invitation," he said in softer tones as he turned his attention back to Caron. "It won't mean your job if you can't come."

"I would love to attend," Caron accepted.

"Good enough!" He lumbered to the door, pausing briefly once more. "I'll send Franklin here to pick you up in one of the cars. About seven?"

"Perfect, sir."

"Bring along an escort," he added on his way out. "Can't have a lady like you out on the streets alone at night."

Once the door separated Ramsey and his man from the attorneys, the glass-walled room began to hum.

"If that old guy wasn't such an important client," Sharp muttered between clenched teeth.

"I'm beginning to think the whole gruff act is a charade to ensure his controlling hand," Caron speculated.

"Regardless, you certainly know how to smooth his feathers," William Peterson admitted. "Keep up the good work, Caron."

"If only he hadn't made that announcement to the press," Sharp complained. He'd wandered back to the table and was leafing through the file on Ramsey.

Caron shrugged. "He's accustomed to running the show. And the show wasn't big enough in his eyes."

"We've got to resolve this heir question one way or the other before this tops Barnum and Bailey," Peterson said.

"The wily old coot's got us performing before a worldwide audience with his million-dollar challenge. Satisfy him, Caron, and in the words of a great book, 'you'll be put in charge of greater affairs.' Whatever you do, follow down each and every lead meticulously."

Caron closed her eyes with a satisfied grin. The message was music to her ears: clean up this crazy controversy and you'll move up in the firm. Her smile soon faded as Rick Wyatt's image floated into view behind her lids. Common sense told her that he never would've called without a concrete reason. Common sense told her that he was one heck of a lead. Why, oh why, did she always put so much stock in common sense?

"WHY ARE YOU SO LATE, Caron?" Megan complained at eight o'clock that evening upon her roommate's return to the town house. "I've been waiting for hours to hear about Hotshot."

Caron trudged across the kitchen linoleum, wrinkling her nose at her rambunctious pal seated at the table wolfing down a huge waffle. Their opposite working hours caused mealtime havoc. Caron occasionally joined Megan in her dinnertime breakfasts, Megan sometimes joined her in a more traditional meal. Ofttimes each fended for herself. This was going to be one of those independent nights for Caron. Her tense stomach was the size of a grape, sparing room for only a cup of coffee which she slid onto the table as she sank into a chair.

Megan frowned at Caron's wrinkled suit jacket. "Rick put ya in the spin cycle or what?"

"Very funny," Caron griped, gulping as the sweet smell of Megan's maple syrup invaded her nostrils. "Why don't you get a daytime job like everybody else? Eat a nice big hamburger at this time of night?"

"Because I'm not like anybody else." Megan hungrily sliced into the waffle.

Caron waited for Megan to stuff her mouth with food before telling her the news. "I didn't speak to Rick yet. Just didn't have the time."

Megan chomped hard and fast in an effort to swallow and speak. Caron took the opportunity to further excuse herself. "I spent the afternoon in court with my sexual discrimination suit and did some after-hours interviewing concerning the baby."

"Darn you, Caron!" Megan finally squawked with a gulp. "Don't you have any news?"

Caron sipped her coffee with a rueful grin. "Well, you wouldn't believe some of the heirlooms people brought in, trying to prove a link to the Ramsey clan."

"Just think, offering a million bucks for a relative," Megan marveled in disbelief. "I'd gladly give him one of mine at half the price."

"I've got a social-climbing mother to contribute myself," Caron tossed in. "Free of charge."

"None of the papers specified what the heirloom is, did they?"

"All I know is that it's a medal of some kind," Caron confided. "Confidential info, by the way."

"Sure, sure," Megan pooh-poohed with a wave of her fork. "So what did you see?"

"Along with tired, hungry babies of all shapes and sizes, I saw trophies, photographs, crystal—things that people pass along through generations. Some of the more notable efforts were a hood ornament from an old Thunderbird, a chunk of gold, a bronzed baby shoe, and my all-time favorite of the night, a suit of armor."

"What a bunch of hustlers," Megan uttered in awe.

Caron flashed her a lopsided grin. "Lots of wishful thinkers anyway. An unusual number of grandmothers brought in their grandsons. Babies they believed couldn't be the seed of certain disappointing males, I guess."

Megan giggled. "Desperate flights to cloud nine."

Caron laughed along. "A million dollars does tend to send the imagination soaring."

"So, after all your interviewing, are you any closer to an answer?"

"No, just more determined to speak to Rick."

"So, go get 'em, tiger!"

Caron squeezed her eyes shut, summoning inner strength. "What if I don't have what it takes to wrangle with him anymore?" she wondered just above a whisper.

"You wrangle for a living now, you idiot!" Megan said with her own brand of bolstering. "You are a *litigator*."

"It's still hard for me with him," Caron despaired, burying her face in her hands. "Can you believe it? One minute on the phone and I was a fat girl with the self-esteem of a peanut."

Megan clucked patiently, accustomed to soothing Caron's self-doubts. "You were never really fat. Just plump. And you have to face him," she insisted, prying Caron's fingers from her delicate features.

Caron rued her fate. "I'm going tonight. Going to see how they do their laundry on the wild side." She sighed wistfully. "Maybe I'll be the prettier one this time."

"Naw, that's too much to expect," Megan predicted. "I'll bet he's still muscle-rippling gorgeous. With that thick black hair, those long sweeping lashes."

"Megan?"

"Yeah?" she asked with a moony grin.

"I wouldn't make any more bets concerning Hotshot. You've yet to clear your tab as it is."

"Get out of town." Megan drained her milk glass and set it down with a thump.

"And I will be the prettier," Caron vowed with a feline grin. "After the jolt he gave me this morning, I figure it's only fair play to stun him out of his senses."

THERE WAS A GODDESS in his Laundromat.

Rick Wyatt had bolted out of the back room of Hotshots, freezing at the sight of the beautiful stranger near the front of the cluttered, machine-filled room. He'd been elbow deep in his own personal affairs, originally coming out to retrieve . . . What? His mind drew a blank slate as he gawked at her in amazement. The place occasionally held a straggler at this time of night, someone who hadn't timed their washload to coincide with his closing time of ten o'clock. But this babe had no laundry, unless she was carrying it inside the red clutch purse tucked under her arm.

A quick, sharp glance to the large-faced clock on the wall told him it was half-past ten now. Apparently he hadn't locked the door. Or had he? Maybe she was an apparition, one manifested by an imaginative man hungry for a good night's sleep.

"Baby, baby, baby," he uttered to himself, quaking in his Nikes. "Tonight's the night . . ."

Rick squinted for a better look, frustrated that the only bulb left burning was the small yellow nightlight over the front door. Flesh or smoke, she was something to see, a long cool beauty leaning a streamlined hip against dryer number seven. He drank in the small hat sitting atop her short cloud of chestnut hair, then skimmed on to her magnificent body, a striking reed in a red-and-blue blocked suit with yellow lapels. Rick, a self-proclaimed man of vanity and virility, was suddenly conscious of his own clothing: snug, tattered jeans and a faded green T-shirt.

What would she think?

Was she even for real?

Maybe his thrill-seeking libido had created her luscious shell. If so, he'd done a bang-up job!

With a deep fortifying breath, he spoke. "I, ah, didn't hear you come in."

She lifted a rich, sable brow. "I'm light on my feet."

He took a step forward, hands clasped behind his back. "We're closed. Have been since ten."

"The door was unlocked."

Was she or wasn't she? he wondered, raking shaky fingers through his hair. "I just don't get it. My bell didn't even ring. It always rings."

A small smile curved her cherry red lips. "Maybe your bell is broken."

"Yeah, maybe." With a burst of determination Rick strutted down the left aisle, past the pool table, past the pop machine, all the while watching her. He knew he'd be bursting the bubble of his own making if she vanished as mysteriously as she'd appeared, but he had to know for sure. He stepped up to the glass door, putting a power grip on the small brass knob. She was still leaning into old number seven, not dissolving into the scuffed tiled floor, not evaporating into the detergent-tinged air.

Hot damn! He was close to her now.

She was real all right. Further scrutiny under the single tubular bulb now centered over his head highlighted her curvy proportions in a golden hue. She was a three-dimensional babe with startling bone structure. Artistic cheeks and dirty dancing-honed hips. The package was wrapped in fabric that had never crossed his threshold empty or otherwise.

Downtown Hotshot meets Uptown Hot Babe. Determined to check the bell, he tugged the sticky door open with a single yank. Cool night air streamed inside to a merry jingle of welcome. Rick's system was jingling too, like a ribbon of sleigh bells. So how'd she get in without him hearing? He filled his lungs with invigorating night air, hoping to stabilize himself. It was a long moment before he shoved the door back into place with a slam and a clang.

"Losing your touch, Hotshot?"

Rick's head jerked back. There was an unmistakable familiarity in her taunt. An intimacy. He pensively rubbed his thin black mustache, not recalling ever being intimate with a goddess.

Rick rapped a knuckle on dryer number one and marched toward number seven, his eyes never once leaving her face as he counted off each machine. Her smile deepened the closer he approached, dimples miraculously forming in the hollows of those sculptured cheeks. It was impossible. Yet . . . "Caron?"

"As if you didn't know," she retorted, slapping her purse down on the dryer behind her.

Rick shook his head in undisguised awe. "It's been ten years, Caron."

"Why, you just talked to me this morning," she said, her voice slipping a notch.

"You happen to sound different in bed," he tossed back, his mouth curling mischievously. "Husky, croaky." He sauntered close, satisfaction warming his gut as she flushed over the innuendo. She deserved it after sneaking up on him this way. "I truly didn't recognize you until you called me Hotshot," he confessed on a more merciful note.

"Maybe it's because I've lost twenty pounds and replaced my glasses with contacts," she suggested, acutely aware of his heart-pounding proximity. Only inches shorter than Rick, she could face him squarely atop her high heels. She was determined to do so, just as she'd done without hesitation in the old days. Why did it seem more difficult now? Was it the sensuous gleam in his dark brown eyes, those arresting features, sharpened with age into flawless balance? His face was as beautiful as a macho man's could be. Good thing, considering his ego would no doubt accept nothing less.

"Ah yes, the Quick Draw wit," he acquiesced. "Sharpened to perfection on poor slugs like me, for the ultimate altruistic goal of saving butt after butt in court." Rick silently roved her face, mesmerized by the glitter of green in her eyes. Those sparklers, filled with vitality and promise, had led him on a merry chase throughout his boyhood. Now they were full of womanly knowledge. If she knew then what she no doubt knew now . . . He shuddered to think of the consequences.

"You are staring at me, Rick."

"You want me to."

"Flirty fool," she scoffed, blinking in disbelief as he raised a large hand to her face and began to trace his finger down the slope of her surgically perfected nose.

"This is new, too."

"Yes," she said breathlessly, acutely aware of the texture of his fingertip. His touch actually made her knees quake. If only she'd worn a longer skirt to hide in, she fretted, as his gaze fell to survey her from head to toe.

When his eyes lifted once again, they were penetrating and demanding. "Why are you here, Caron?"

"You called me." She kept her head high, knowing that the drop from his eye to his belt would be like falling from the frying pan they'd discussed earlier, straight into the flames. She'd already noticed that those ragged jeans of his still held the tightest rear end on the planet. "We have to talk about a certain baby," she stated. "A baby I think we both care about."

"Do you think we could possibly be on the same side of an issue for once?" he asked in mocking amazement.

Caron was aghast. "Of course we are! I want nothing more than for that sweet, defenseless boy to get what's coming to him."

Rick's mouth curved in a secret smile of satisfaction. "Right answer, counselor. You must really wow 'em in court with that delivery."

"I've had my moments," she agreed airily. "It's easier to get a point across without you there, contradicting my every word."

"Too bad I didn't follow you into the legal profession." He rubbed his square, stubbled chin. "We could've wallowed in continual debate and gotten paid for the pleasure."

She shook her head, her shiny brown cap of hair swinging around her face. "You are still the most exasperating boy I've ever known."

His deep, masculine chuckle echoed hollowly through the room. "Wrong answer, this time. This rebel's a man now."

3

OH, YES. RICK WYATT was a man now. Caron closed her eyes briefly against his smug smile, made more roguish these days by the black mustache now etched across his upper lip. She sought to still the quiver running the length of her before it visibly shook her in her high heels. A cool head was needed here. He'd seen right through her bid for attention. The moment would be his if she backed down even an inch. How many times in the past had he edged in close, dominating her with his sheer physical strength, his irresistible magnetism?

A million times.

Hotshot had turned her to putty whenever it suited him. Whenever he wanted something. Early on it had been the wheels from her buggy for his go-cart, nickels to round off his dollar. Later it was a cookie from her bag lunch, notes from literature class, hand-sewn seat covers for his old jalopy.

But the stakes were higher now. A billion times higher. With her precious job in the center of it all. If she botched this baby deal, she'd be out of a job, her reputation as a competent attorney at serious risk.

She was his putty only if she allowed herself to be.

Acknowledging his methods on an intellectual level didn't stop her fragile emotions from responding to him on a sexual plane. It was nearly impossible to reason with his sturdy broad-chested form hovering so very, very close. The fabric of his shirt was threadbare and pulled taut across his chest, enticingly outlining every muscle. A weightlifter's body. A young woman's dream. A precarious spot for a lady lawyer who relied so heavily on her powers of reason!

"Rick, you are invading my space," she accused.

"Caron, you are presently in my space," he differed. "Back on my turf of your own free will." He stepped closer, grunting in satisfaction as her bottom backed into old number seven, wedging her neatly between him and the dryer with a distinctive thump.

Caron's heart was beating a fierce tattoo now. Allowing him to corner her had been a mistake.

As his mouth curled into a lusty grin, she recalled its taste with sharp, surprising clarity. From where had the memory of their fledgling kisses materialized? They'd experimented with make-out techniques during the hot, sultry days of their fourteenth summer. Caron could still feel his lips, his tongue, the way his fingers raked her hair. It had been new, exciting, forbidden. Rick had been her friend, her wonderful, funny confidant during that summer of growth, that journey from child to teenager.

But once across the bridge, Rick had broken into a sprint. He'd gone on to experiment with every girl in reach. That bygone summer had drawn out their strong points, ultimately separating them because of their sharp contrasts. Puberty had brought Rick's virility and cocky indifference into sharp focus, as well as Caron's high IQ and knack for studies. Oh, how she'd wanted to tell the world she'd been in a three-month lip-lock with Rick Wyatt. But by the first snowfall, she was sure no one would believe her. She was the brain. The bookworm. The plump girl with the premature bustline. Rick Wyatt was . . . Hotshot. And he apparently didn't like the new her. Not enough to continue those kissing games . . .

"I had expected some sort of response from your end," he admitted silkily, grazing her arm with his as he propped a hand on number seven. "Something in the form of nipping legal hounds. Waited all day for them."

The naughty curl to her mouth confirmed she'd been sorely tempted to send in the cavalry. "I'm here because I think we can do better than that phone conversation. After all, our days of debating dress codes and dance bands and hall passes are long over. We are adults."

"I did call with high hopes, of course." Resting his hip on dryer six, he reached over to toy with her little yellow hat, shifting its angle on her head. "But we still debate with intensity from opposite poles."

In other words, he was still shaping the rules to suit him. Fiddling with her hat as he gave her the brush, too! His audacity on both fronts made her blood boil. "Just like that, eh?" she snapped, brushing aside his busy hands. "You involve yourself in a billion-dollar destiny and just say oops, not for me after all."

"My final decision was made with a little more effort than oops," he assured her. "I am more than brawn these days. Not nearly as brainy as you, but I get along."

If Caron didn't know better, she'd have thought there was a defensive edge to his tone. But it just couldn't be. To her knowledge, Rick hadn't had an uncertain moment in his entire childhood. And probably not in manhood, either.

Rick heaved a sigh of resignation. "Calling you was a regrettable mistake, Caron."

A mistake. That stung Caron deep. They'd been so close once. True, they'd never officially dated. He'd never even called her, not even once to cinch the bet with Megan. But their mental sparring over the years had been so intimate, so sexy, that she couldn't stand it that he didn't want her still. Not even with her new foxy look. "So much for old friends," she muttered in disappointment.

Rick reared back in surprise as she shifted the blame on him. "You wanted me to jump through your law-and-order hoops before you'd even talk to me. Treated me like a cocky kid who didn't know what was best for him."

Caron's mouth sagged open. "The last time we spoke you were a cocky kid, Rick."

Realization sheeted his face, defusing his temper. "Guess it has been that long. I will admit I was the terror of the neighborhood back then, the guy all mothers feared. Daughters were shoved into basements and under beds when I walked down the street." Humor twitched his jaw. "And I guess that's what made the challenge to win each and every one irresistible."

Caron's mother, Deborah, had been among those with one hand on her daughter and the other on the basement light switch. It hadn't stopped Caron, or any of the other girls, however, from flitting in and out of Rick's reach.

"A mature adult stands before you," he asserted passionately. "I'm continually working to prove myself worthy of this very neighborhood where I caused all the havoc. I love it here so much, Caron." His face lit up as he scanned his kingdom of a utility room with open fondness. "This is my investment in the good life, helping folks in need, befriending the local kids. It's especially satisfying to be here for the lonely ones who don't have the happy home life I had." Rick placed a hand on her shoulder. "Don't you think I'm making a difference, even if I'm not a stockbroker or a scientist?"

Expressing his importance, his purpose in life, seemed so urgent to him. Caron didn't know what to make of it. Since when was he unsure of his path? He'd glided along on good looks and savvy his whole life, hadn't he? "Rick, I'm sure you're a rousing success," she obliged.

His heavy brows arched in hope. "You really think so?"

All she could think about were his fingertips digging into the silky fabric of her color-blocked jacket, into the flesh of her shoulder. It sent streaks of heat through her body, driving all rational thought to the wayside. She twisted free of his trap with a breathless tug. "Don't, Rick."

"Maybe you should go, Caron," he suggested quietly. "I know now you can't help me."

"I just can't walk away," she explained in stubborn apology, her feet rooted to the floor. "You're . . . You happen to be . . ." She stumbled to express herself.

"Quick Draw lost for words?" he asked mockingly, looming over her willowy body, larger than life itself.

She pursed her lips in aggravated surrender. "You just happen to be my first solid lead."

"I am?"

"Well, you don't have to be so downright delighted about it," she bristled.

"I'm sorry," he offered in suspect sincerity. "You've always been so capable. Who'd have ever guessed you'd end up on my doorstep in need of anything!"

"We seem to need each other," she pointed out. "Obviously James Ramsey was part of this neighborhood family you are so fond of. I'll bet you were great pals who shared lots of confidences."

Rick rolled his eyes to the ceiling, as if about to surrender Valley Forge. "Okay, he was a good friend. We are still grieving his death around here."

"I am sorry for your loss," she offered softly. "Just give me a little more to go on, and I'll be out of here."

"One scoop in my arms and you'd be outta here too," he threatened.

Caron tried to ignore the storm growing in his manner. "What about the mother? At least tell me where she is."

"The mother is not an issue at this point."

"She should stand up and be counted immediately," Caron warned practically, "so Douglas Ramsey doesn't plow right over her."

"So he does live up to James's description," Rick muttered. "I won't allow him to treat the heir as a little possession straight from a cabbage patch with no history, no ties."

"The old man has a heart on some levels," Caron hastily assured. "He just needs to be shown the way. How to love unconditionally."

"I don't think he deserves an heir."

Caron could barely contain her amazement. Rick sure saw himself at the center of the controversy, pulling all the strings. But how like him with his ego, to fancy himself at the helm of this baby search. Adding him to the head count with Douglas Ramsey and herself, that brought the number of chiefs to three! She ached to probe on, find out just how this streetwise rebel ended up fighting this billion-dollar cause, but she checked herself promptly. If he blew up, he *would* scoop her up and deposit her on the street! With her luck, some old neighbor would be passing by in the dead of night and promptly call her mother!

As Caron stared into Rick's dark eyes full of emotion and strength, she recalled Megan's earlier remark about the guts it must've taken for him to call her at all. There had to be some tremendous intent behind it. She thought back to how he'd approached her, before the bantering got heated. "You said you were looking for someone reliable," she ventured, trying not to grit her teeth over the description. "I still am, Rick. Always will be."

Rick rubbed his chin, studying the floor. "Well, I had this plan.... Maybe I just hoped you'd be complacent—like many of the other women I know."

Caron erupted in a surprised laugh. "No, I guess I'm still not the pliable sort you've always desired most."

Rick appeared ready to argue, then thought better of it. "If it were to be carried out, it would have to be done so immediately. The closer Ramsey gets, the quicker the clock ticks."

"Huh?"

"Never mind that for now," he directed. "What I originally had in mind was to use your position to get me into Ramsey territory. I planned to personally check out this billionaire grandfather, make sure he wouldn't disrupt the boy's life."

Caron gasped in disbelief. "You really intended to take that powerful man for a test spin?"

"Why not?" Rick folded his arms across his chest, as still and sturdy as a mighty tree trunk. "He plans to take the potential heir for one, doesn't he?"

"Perhaps, in a way," Caron conceded, fingering her hat. Rick still had an uncanny insight concerning people. Persons other than herself, anyway. "It would be impossible to get close to a man like him without arousing his suspicion."

"It would've looked natural if you'd introduced me as your old school pal, as James's laundryman."

Rick's voice was casual, but his idea held a well-thought-out ring to Caron, someone who weighed her words in court down to the ounce. "He has built a department store empire on gut and instinct, something you understand quite well, Rick. It would be tough to hoodwink him."

"People see what they want to see, especially when they're desperate. It's the delivery that counts the most sometimes. Right, counselor?"

"Touché for courtroom tactics," she relented, rankled that he could still bring her down on the verbal mat with a sound smack, despite their maturity.

"So, those *would have* been my terms," he said expectantly."

"What was I to gain?" she demanded.

His gaze clouded. "I can't tell you yet, not exactly."

"My job would be on the line and you can't confide your motives?"

Rick threw up his hands in a flare of temper. "I knew we couldn't get it together! The whole damn state is looking for this kid and you're not sure you can risk letting downtown Wyatt here mingle with the upper crust." He seized her upper arms, giving her a gentle shake. "Let go and trust me, Caron. I can breeze in and out for the facts, before he knows what hit him." He searched her stoic features for any signs of a meltdown.

Caron struggled to hold her cool. "This search is my responsibility. My big chance for bigger things."

"Take a chance on me. The beginning of the tunnel is dark, but it is a shortcut for you. You see, Caron, no matter how many avenues you search, they all lead back here to Fairfax. Back to me."

His arrogance scalded her. "Really, Rick? Surely there must be a detour around the mighty you! Someone else in this business district, for instance, must know the whereabouts of that child!"

He rubbed the back of his neck with a weary sigh. "Like it or not we are joined at the hip on this one. I've got the info you need. You've got the influence with Douglas Ramsey I need. I'm smart enough to know he wouldn't buy my arriving at the stately manor one day just to chat about his son. He'd check me out, probe into things that are none of his business. The kid could never get away once the old guy knew his identity. That's what seems so unfair."

"Why must I wait for your information?"

"Because it's better for you," he said to her surprise. "If everything were to blow, you'd have an honest ticket out. Ignorance."

Everything could blow? Why oh why did Rick's life always seem larger than life itself? And how in the world had he managed to make his selfish offer sound downright gallant? "So you want my blind trust? The chance to run loose in my life?"

He shrugged, his angled jaw twitching. "Well, yeah. We trusted each other as kids, didn't we? Shared everything. Especially in the early days."

Caron's hand stole to her mouth, causing him to chuckle knowingly. He knew she was remembering the kissing games. She reddened, instantly dropping her fingertips from her lips as though they were red-hot to the touch.

Rick's lips proved even hotter than hers. With a finger hooked under her chin, he was impulsively kissing her, hot, hard and deep. He was experimenting as he used to, but with a whole lot more expertise.

And it felt so good. Her body liquefied in her shoes as she drank from his taste, his scent. No other male had ever made her insides quiver in a simple lip-lock. With a single feather-light crook to her chin he was thoroughly ravaging her mouth with driving force. She knew he was making a deliberate point, showing her just how profound their chemistry was.

She needed no such reminder.

He'd spoiled every simple smooch for every man after him a long time ago.

She finally broke the union, stumbling out to the aisle. "I just can't go along with you blindly," she whispered on a steadying breath.

"You just did."

Rick's triumphant grin convinced Caron that while he may be a special friend to many a kid in the neighborhood, he was certainly no humble Father Flannagan. She busily collected her purse, and her hat, which had somehow ended up on the floor. "This search is serious, Rick."

"You are still just too serious in general, Quick Draw. I was trying to show you that."

"My terms are simple enough," she stated briskly. "Give me something to believe in, or I'm out of here."

"Believe in me."

If Caron could only believe in those eyes, suddenly haunted with some secret yearning. That mouth, wavering the line between compassion and resentment. But Rick had let her down once with a crushing blow that still pained her at times. She just couldn't surrender without something. Anything. "You were right," she conceded quietly. "This conversation has nowhere to go. So, I'll just be going."

"It doesn't all come from books," Rick called after her retreating figure. "Just remember who taught you how to kiss."

Caron froze on her heel near the door, whirling back in fury. "Just remember who taught you right back. Who gave you the experience to go on and confidently kiss every girl in sight." She was gone then. Out the door with a slam and a clang.

"YOU HAVE GROWN into one major distraction, Bobber."

Up in his apartment above the Laundromat five minutes later, Rick regarded his companion with a tsk and a sigh. With capable hands he lifted the drowsy baby from its molded infant seat, gently resting him against his chest. He sat down in the rocker near the picture window facing the street, shifting the child in his arms so he could talk with him face-to-face. "My bell rang down there in the shop and for the first time in four years, I didn't hear it. How can you have me so hypnotized?"

Bobber's white moon-shaped face brightened at the playful timbre of Rick's voice, his lopsided grin of exasperation. "Anyway, thanks for not letting out a war whoop from the stockroom. I would've made the proper introductions. But as it was, buddy, she was absolutely too sassy to deserve it. Still, I gotta confess," he relented in a sigh, "seeing her in the flesh after all these years set the old heart to thumpin'."

The baby jammed a fat fist in his mouth, his blue saucer eyes wide and inquisitive. As Rick rambled on, the baby sucked on, drool rolling down between the folds of his double chin.

"I know what you're thinking, Bobber. Yesterday I said I could pull her into the caper with no trouble at all, if she had the guts to come within smooching range. Well, I did it. Kissed her, I mean. But there is obviously a limit to the hotshot magic. Male arrogance is the culprit here, my boy. Avoid letting it run your life once your drooling days are over."

Rick sighed again, running his thumbs through the baby's fine red hair. "No matter what, the law firm will be zooming in on this street within days, considering all the time James spent around here. That's why I've got you stashed away, isn't it, buddy? Of course, Ramsey's million-dollar reward is going to accelerate the law firm's investigation. That's what finally gave me the courage to call Caron this morning. A call I've been putting off for a week.

She was my only hope of getting a sneak peek at Ramsey before he gets one of us."

Rick stared off into space for a moment, reliving their kiss, chock-full of unfulfilled passions and promises. Their mutual needs would remain in ungratified limbo it seemed. Though the static was still there, aged to high voltage. The air was thick with it, before they touched. Before they even spoke! he realized in retrospect.

Their desires were a ticking ten-year time bomb bound to explode before the heir controversy was settled once and for all. It was a certainty, because she would be back. Not right away, of course. She'd turn over every leaf in the neighborhood, drill every potential heir who marched into her office with a claim. Her pride would keep her sniffing out every clue around him. But she would ultimately return. He hoped it would be in time to still go ahead with his plan.

Bobber released a contented coo as Rick drew him back to his shoulder and rocked to and fro in the creaky old chair. "Sure, I would've liked nothing better than to take her into my confidence, Bob. Back in the really old kissing-game days I told her everything. But that was before she blossomed into a young woman, an articulate scholar. Of course, there were some high times after that, when I thought maybe I could match wits with her, regain the special bond we once had. But even taking on the student council presidency didn't give me enough mental prowess to overtake her for anything lasting. Even the prom ended badly. My last chance with the only girl who'd ever challenged me a whit. I walked away with a sandwich in my cummerbund. That's class, Bob. With a capital C."

Rick grinned as Bobber gurgled in an effort to join in. "You're right, man. I have to concentrate on our billion-dollar mission. Our news is big, Bob. And it can't be hushed up again once out of the bag. We owe it to James to follow his instructions. No matter how hot a babe is, a man's loyalty to a dying wish is top priority.

"Ah, you should've known her back then," Rick murmured, growing groggy himself from the motion of the chair. "She had a unique round beauty in the old days. A verbal pistol, but somehow warm and humane, too. I don't understand why she went and took such a stuffy job. Or why she had that silly nose job. There was something quite nice about it the way it was. . . .

THE SILHOUETTE OF MAN and baby in the apartment window, gently rocking together in a bath of yellow lamplight, made a moving picture on the street below. Caron stared at the red brick building for the longest time, finding it difficult to tear herself away from the touching scene.

She'd been sitting behind the wheel of her blue Saturn collecting her thoughts, when a light had flicked on in the picture window above the Laundromat. Caron hadn't known it was Rick's apartment until he moved into view, seating himself in the rocker with the baby. She'd drawn the key away from the ignition, frozen at the wheel.

So much for faith! The wily lout had the baby in his possession the whole time. Even though she'd pleaded for some gesture of good will, he'd remained silent through it all!

Yet, the sight of the pair nipped at her heart. Rick still had the power to send her, all right. She watched his head move in animation, no doubt conversing with the child. A lullaby perhaps? A fairy tale? The baby eventually fell against the wide breadth of his shoulder like a rag doll, at home in the cradle of his sinewy arms.

But that baby wasn't at home at all, she reminded herself, shaking out of her reverie. She was willing to bet her hard-earned sheepskin on it. No wonder Rick didn't want Ramsey to start investigating his personal life. Rick had all the evidence needed to seal the case. A good twenty-five pounds' worth!

"OH CARON!"

Caron halted in the courthouse hallway Thursday morning at her mother's shrill voice. A cursory look around convinced her there was no time to slip behind one of the marble pillars. No time to meld into the bustle of the lunchtime crowd. Deborah Carlisle had her trapped, cornered for the sort of confrontation she called conversation.

"At last!" Deborah, handsomely decked out in a smart beige suit, her dark blond hair cropped and stiff with spray, skidded to a smooth stop before her daughter.

"Hello, Mom," Caron greeted, unconsciously clenching her teeth. Mother and daughter suffered from nature's curse of opposing personalities. Caron's wealth of feelings and her keen sensitivity for her fellow man hovered just beneath the surface. Deborah's nerves of steel and shallow values were buried beneath a buffer of extremely thick skin.

Deborah raised a clutch purse to her small, slightly heaving chest. "Didn't you see me? Didn't you hear me? I was right behind you."

Caron shrugged helplessly, forcing brightness into her tone. "Did you sit in on the trial today?"

"Yes, darling. What a wonderful speech you gave at the end," Deborah enthused, clasping her hands together. "Not one complaint from the other side."

Caron smiled wryly. "Objections aren't permitted during the final argument."

"Of course, of course," Deborah conceded in airy dismissal. "I must say that I'm surprised you didn't notice me in there. You usually do."

Indeed Caron did! Her keen internal defenses usually announced Mother Carlisle's courtroom appearances by drawing to attention the little hairs on the back of Caron's neck. Had since the fraud case where Deborah had stood up to voice an objection to something the judge said. It took some fast talking to avoid a fine that time. Deborah stayed away from court for three blissful weeks.

"It seems to me that asking for thousands of dollars for sexual harassment is a little greedy though, dear," Deborah chided, patting her golden shell of hair.

Caron summoned patience from the depths of her soul. "Mother, if we'd have asked for a quarter, they may have given us just a nickel. Understand?"

Deborah rolled her attractive hazel eyes, sabotaged with a heavy layer of mascara and green shadow. "Heaven knows I try. But the fuss seems so inflated for the crime."

"Mother, my client is in therapy. She's truly suffering." Caron drew a breath as if to continue, then clamped her mouth shut again. Deborah was in true form today and nothing would sway her. She'd never held a job outside the home, but still felt she could put a price tag on the serious charge of harassment in the workplace. But why not? Caron mused sourly. Deborah compulsively put a price tag on everything. Measured all situations by her own set of narrow-minded values and personal value of a dollar.

"Let's talk about something fun," Deborah suggested, raising a finger to Caron's face to fluff the strands of brown hair curving her cheek.

Caron shifted her purse and briefcase from one hand to another in a fidgety movement. She'd been planning to stop by Hotshots while the jury deliberated. Knowing that the baby was there was driving her crazy. But it was the last thing she cared to confide to her mother, who still indulged in negative reminiscences about Hotshot himself. Deborah never forgave him for breezing into Truman High politics with bulging muscles and a flawless face, usurping Caron from the president's position on the student council. "Never cracked a book but always had a charming crack," Mother Carlisle said at the time. She'd spent the year trying to unseat Rick through the faculty to no avail.

Of course, there was the prom incident to cap off the year. Her gentle father had been distressed over the time she'd eventually arrived home. Her mother went wild over the stain on her sateen gown. The price tag had been outrageous, on the dress and on the evening itself. Deborah had ranted to the neighbors afterward, proclaiming it the crowning touch of Rick's high school antics. Caron had crawled into her summer job at the library during the sultry months of controversy. Deborah had milked it for all it was worth, one last hurrah before the class of '83 dispersed into adulthood. Deborah's friendship with Eleanor Wyatt, often on shaky ground because of the children, was utterly destroyed by it. Considering the feud with the Wyatts still stood firm to this day, Caron hoped to keep Rick's connection to the billionaire baby a secret.

"I see you took advantage of the sale at Brooks," Deborah was chirping as she scanned Caron's blue wool blazer and gray A-line skirt, oblivious to Caron's rattled state of mind.

"Yes, I bought this suit and two others."

Deborah lifted a carefully plucked brow. "Something a little jazzy too, I hope."

"You know I need separate outfits for court," she fired back in timeworn explanation. "I did buy something more colorful, though, something I spotted in Reed's window. A bold color-block jacket with a matching miniskirt."

"The one with the yellow lapels?" Deborah asked, cringing her face for the worst.

"Yes, Mom!"

"Yellow doesn't suit you, dear," she said in crisp judgment. "You have a winter complexion."

"This is a lemon yellow, not a gold one."

"Yellows can be tremendously tricky," she maintained dubiously.

"Bought a matching hat, too," Caron confided with a smirk. "Little felt cloche."

"Yellow?"

"Lemony lemon," she confided in exaggerated urgency.

"Oh, my stars." Deborah clapped her own cheeks for effect, careful not to disturb her makeup.

Caron pushed back the sleeve of her blazer and stole a glance at her watch.

Deborah's thin brows arched in discontent. "In a hurry, are you?"

"It is lunchtime," Caron attempted.

"I'd skip a few lunches here and there if you want to wear that block suit well," she advised on the QT, as if masking a family scandal.

"I am in control of my own body," Caron objected in a clear voice. "And skipping meals is no way to stay healthy."

"My daughter the lawyer thinks she's a doctor now!" Deborah lamented. "I've kept this figure for thirty years by munching on lettuce leaves at lunch."

"Nice chatting with you, Mom."

Deborah caught her arm as Caron began to edge into the crowd. She pulled her back with a yank. "You don't even know why I'm here," she chided. "I spent the entire morning thinking of you."

"Mom—"

"It just so happens I bought you a gift," she tempted in singsong. "For Saturday night's affair . . ."

Caron whirled back, her eyes boring into her mother's. "What affair?"

"I know all about your invitation to the Ramsey estate," she returned, pursing her lips smugly. "I stopped by your office this morning looking for you and that nice Mr. Peterson told me all about it."

Caron took delight in mentally placing the talkative partner over a pit of zealous prosecutors.

"This is *the* social gala, my dear daughter," Deborah gushed with reverence. "I overheard a couple of women discussing it at the spa last week. Oh, if only I'd known then that my daughter was going! I'd have told 'em a thing or two!" She paused to scowl. "Of course if your father had better connections at the bank, we'd have our own invitation. He has the salary now, but none of the clout."

"Father is wonderful just the way he is," Caron automatically asserted.

"I'm sure you and the partners have some sort of pre-arrangement," Deborah said pitifully. "No extra tickets, I suppose."

Tickets? Caron grimaced. It wasn't a production of *Hamlet* at the Denver Center of Performing Arts! Of course, to Deborah such an event would be a stage performance. "By invitation only, Mom," she calmly voiced aloud. "You know how social etiquette works."

"Especially for the cream of society. So hard to break in."

Caron had grown accustomed to her mother's thirst for a sip of that cream. When Deborah left the Truman High neighborhood for Raspberry Hills Village, she had high hopes of joining the ranks of the elite. She had managed to finagle and harangue her way up the social ladder a rung or two, but that was all. She was still trying.

"This really is a business affair for the law firm, Mom," she firmly explained. "Douglas Ramsey is a client."

"I read all about that billionaire baby in the papers yesterday," she forged on with a pouty look. "Of course I never figured you to be involved, until Mr. Peterson told me."

"It's been confidential to this point," she protested in excuse.

"But this connection could be priceless to us—you—socially," Deborah chided in excitement. "Caron, you might find the missing baby yourself. To think that you might be the little mite's savior!"

Deborah would explode if she knew that Hotshot had his hands on the baby, that he wished to be master of the boy's fate. Caron suppressed a smirk as she pondered the possibilities. What if Rick ended up with a cool million because he happened to befriend James Ramsey, gain the late man's trust? What if her mother eventually came to the ironic realization that she herself could've made the Ramsey family social connection through James, had she not fled her old neighborhood for the fancy suburbs?

Leaving Deborah to watch the facts unfold in the newspaper in days to come, to sort out the shoulda-beens and coulda-beens all on her own, seemed like the most satisfying and self-preserving thing to do.

"I really must dash now," Caron said.

"All right. You can walk me to my car, feast your eyes on the most exquisite dress ever. You'll never guess the color. Not in a hundred years."

Caron bit her lip. "Rose?"

"Yes, my darling, yes. We'll get it right this time round," her mother assured. "Finally, another night at the ball, my Cinderella. With no padded hips and no permanent punch stains. No Hotshot!" Her rejoicing laughter echoed through the high-ceilinged hallway, causing heads to turn. "Mr. Peterson said you had no date," she mumbled on the downbeat as they approached the elevator.

Caron rolled her eyes. "It's fine with me. I consider it more of a business event than anything else."

"How about that Paul Drake?"

Caron froze in her tracks. "Who, Mother?"

"The pleasant young man who called me the other night looking for your unlisted telephone number."

Caron drew an astonished breath. "So *you* gave it out!"

"He did call at a hideous hour, but such a charming man. And considering it was concerning a high school reunion . . ." she trailed off, as if giving an adequate excuse.

A reunion for two, anyhow! Caron bit her lip hard, swallowing back the laughter. Rick must've called her mother right before he called her.

"Oh, he sounds just delicious," Deborah chattered on, as they stepped into the elevator. "Said he's single and runs his own detective agency in California."

"Certainly a scrumptious catch," Caron concurred wryly. Despite his proclamations of charitable intentions, Rick certainly still had a rebellious streak in him. Imagine, getting her number in the most daring way possible. Pushing Deb's buttons with promises of a reunion to show off Caron's achievements. Intimating his availability as a single professional man. The most mischievous part of the stunt, of course, was introducing himself as Paul Drake, prosperous private detective, knowing full well that Deb would make an utter fool of herself the moment she tried to brag about him to anyone else. Unlike the majority of Americans, her mother had little time for television or mystery novels, so therefore wouldn't recognize the name of Perry Mason's fictional sidekick.

This was just the sort of scam that made Rick shine. He knew it would make her laugh. He was so clever, so street smart. Oh, how anxious she was to get back to his place. Because of the baby, of course!

4

IT WAS NEARLY four o'clock that afternoon when Caron finally pulled her Saturn into an angled parking slot in front of Hotshots. She sat back for a moment to catch her breath, to think back on the times when she'd been among the teenagers on the sidewalk lining the strip of storefronts.

The area looked older in the stark sunlight, older than it had during her school days, older than it had under last night's cover of darkness. Still, the shops were well kept. Rick's Laundromat was positioned between an ancient music store whose window was still plastered with posters featuring the latest trends in tunes, and Marshall's Market, the mom and pop headquarters for after-school snacks and milk on the run. Rick's building had originally housed a shoe store patronized by the elderly. Clever Hotshot certainly had had a vision when he transformed it into a thriving business, catering to all ages, judging by those entering and exiting.

Some things had changed, some things had not.

Despite the fact that the jury had deliberated only two short hours over her sexual harassment case, delivering a very favorable verdict on behalf of her client, despite the fact that she was dressed in one of her power suits, Caron still felt every bit as insecure as the students now passing by her windshield no doubt did.

Rick Wyatt made her feel that way! she inwardly lamented, rapping the dashboard with disgust. His insensitive treatment of yesterday, along with her mother's callous insistence that she was never good enough, were the seeds that made her the insecure woman she was today.

But she was pretty enough! Logic told her so over and over again. Megan told her so as well.

Caron had no illusions of ever being able to straighten out her mother. But Rick was another matter entirely. Enticing him into pursuit, solid proof of her desirability, would be the ultimate triumph. She'd tossed and turned the night away analyzing her own motives and feelings. The slinky suit had been—though rather unconsciously—the first move in a strategy for seduction. She wanted to reach Hotshot on a purely animal level. Prove to both of them that she was too beautiful for him to resist. In her mind, this would cancel out his rejection years ago. She was getting to him already. It seemed to be on a purely angry level, but at least he was thinking about her. . . .

Caron's frivolous mission was completely out of her sensible character. But the notion of blowing him out of the water had escalated steadily in her mind since his call. She wanted to down him so badly her ears nearly rang from the pressure. If she finally managed to make herself his obsession, she'd never feel unattractive again. She'd have conquered the best.

But there was the baby to consider first and foremost. With effort, she turned her thoughts back to the business at hand. An innocent boy's future depended upon her.

Caron eluded the heat of the October sunshine by ducking under Rick's brown-fringed awning. The large canvas cover, obviously fashioned for the cowhide look, had apparently been folded up last night, escaping her attention. Suddenly it occurred to her that the inside of the place was nothing but a dark, murky memory of machines and shadows. Blending in with a cluster of giggly girls, she tried to peek through the front windowpane. Wooden slat blinds tilted shut made it impossible, however. Just desserts, considering that her energies had been funneled into being the scenery, not absorbing it. Summoning courage on a deep breath, Caron turned the knob and gave the sticky wooden door a shove.

The bell didn't jingle into an intimate, quiet room this time. Her entrance was lost in the hubbub of bright lights, laughter-laced chatter and grinding machines.

She certainly wouldn't be striking a provocative pose on dryer number seven again, she thought with a look at the machine. It was currently being stuffed full of undershirts by a potbellied man with more hair in his ears than on his head.

So this was Rick's wonderland during visitor's hours. She rotated on her heel, drinking in the western motif. Who'd have ever imagined Hotshot to be a closet cowboy beneath his old leather jacket and streetwise lingo? Yet, in the light of day, there was no denying the Colorado country theme of the huge carnival of a room. The walls of knotty pine served as the backdrop for an elk's head, prairie sketches and a variety of wood and stone bric-a-brac. The slow twang of a Willie Nelson ballad erupted from ceiling speakers, crackling along with the tuneless drone of the machines.

Had she ever really known him? The uncertainty made this moment even tougher. Caron liked predictability. She prepared all of her moves as she did for her cases, with meticulous caution.

Caron soon realized that Rick had meant it when he said that he controlled all the moves on his turf. He was standing near the washers, enchanting the socks—and Lord only knew what else—off a tight circle of females. Duded up in black jeans, a red-and-black plaid shirt and scuffed black boots, he was definitely dressed for show. No matter how strong his detergent, how amusing his roomful of games, Hotshot himself was the major attraction. It reminded her of the way he'd held court in the Truman High halls. Hip and sexy, spouting all the right lines. As his rich laughter floated up into the soap-scented air, Caron wondered if anyone ever really changed under the skin. Could he be the sensitive, caring man he claimed?

"Still have your girls, I see."

Rick's head snapped up as he caught her teasing salvo above the din. He regarded her with a measure of surprise over the top of a fiftyish blonde. Something crossed his chocolate brown eyes beneath those luxuriant black lashes. Hope? Anticipation?

"Just demonstrating how a spritz of hair spray can remove ink from cotton," he announced. He turned back to his women to add, "Blot with a towel and add it to your load."

"Aren't you Deb's daughter?" a feminine voice abruptly exclaimed.

Caron turned to find her former next-door neighbor standing behind her. "How are you, Mrs. Bernside?" she asked, delightedly clasping the older woman's hand.

"Just fine, Caron. My, my, you've turned out lovely," she said after a head-to-toe inspection. "Simply lovely."

"Thank you," Caron murmured, a warm tug at her heart. This was a woman who had on many occasions listened to her dreams, her fears, fulfilling the patient caretaking role her own mother never could quite master. "How's Sharon?" she asked, inquiring after Mrs. Bernside's daughter.

"She and Dean have given me two darling grandchildren," Judy proudly reported.

Caron began to pick out other familiar faces in the circle of stain students. They were the mothers of her former classmates, the same women who had disliked and feared Rick, who had made every attempt to shield their precious daughters from him. Now they were patronizing his place, hanging out right along with the new generation of kids! Perhaps he had truly turned over a new leaf. Or perhaps this was the challenge of a lifetime for an amorous con artist with a chip on his shoulder.

"Hey, Rick, you gotta get this babe!" a skinny teenage boy with yellow hair called out from the air hockey table against the back wall. "Can't ruin your record, man."

"He'll come through," his small, dark competitor chimed in, giving the blonde a high five above the table.

Caron folded her arms across her chest, lifting her chin as Rick swaggered her way with group approval. Ever so slowly he rolled up one plaid sleeve, then the other, over his thick forearms. He was peeling back power, sinewy muscle under taut, hair-dusted skin.

This wasn't going at all as she'd planned it. He was already calling the shots again, as he had with their kiss last night. Hoping to escape, she jerked her eyes up to his face. Another trap, she realized with heart-stopping fright as they locked into a single intense beam of his 'n' hers.

His eyes were full of surprise most of all. Naturally he hadn't expected her back so soon. But what disturbed her was the mischief twinkling in their chocolate depths. He was up to something that was going to leave her putty once more.

"Rick . . ." she trailed off in hushed warning.

"Relax," he murmured under his breath. "Trust is a two-way street. If I'm gonna give some, I'm gonna get some, too." He paused for a beat, giving her a chance to dart for the exit if she wished. When she stood her ground, he turned to the boys. "Hit it!"

One of the hockey players in back dropped a quarter in the jukebox and to Caron's amazement, streams of a lively fiddle number crackled through speakers overhead.

Rick grasped Caron by the hand and yanked her to his body. She stopped short against his solid torso with a thud.

"What are you trying to pull?" she squeaked for his ears only.

"Back off a little, Caron," he chided good-humoredly, wrapping an arm around her waist over the bulk of her wool blazer. "You're too anxious."

"Anxious? Me?" Caron was fuming, steeping like a little teapot about to blow its delicate porcelain top. This was ridiculous! She hadn't come to give a show. She was about to set him straight, when his mouth slanted in a roguish grin. He already knew she hated this display. Just as sure as he was a closet cowboy!

"This is the two-step tradition here at Hotshots," he explained calmly. "The Hotshot himself is expected to dance with each and every new lady customer."

"What if I say no?"

"Then you will be the first."

The crowd was cheering them now. Rick took the initiative, swiftly sweeping her into motion, steering down the front aisle lined with dryers.

"Still all fun and games," she griped, following his lead the best she could. A jumble of sensations surged through her, pumping her heart all the harder. Everyone had stepped back to provide a path, even the man at dryer number seven. They clapped to the beat as Rick whisked her along, forcing her to draw her feet up and down off the floor with his. As they passed by the boys in back, the dark-haired one set a worn straw cowboy hat on Rick's head.

"Whimsy is as necessary to humans as water and air," he chided in her ear. "All those years in school and you still haven't learned that simple lesson."

Caron's cry of rebuttal was lost in her throat as Rick whirled her around smartly. Hoots and howls rewarded the tricky maneuver.

"See, Caron, everybody loves a good show," he claimed proudly between breaths. She was puffing a bit herself, taken aback by the absurdity of the moment, the physical demands of the dance and Rick's downright earthy mystique.

In spite of her determination and well-tuned cardiovascular system, Caron lost her footing as they sashayed around the counter holding the cash register. Her heel accidentally landed on his instep, and she toppled into him in a breathless heap. He stopped short with a grunt of pain, his hands closing at her waist to right her.

"I didn't mean it," she said as they stood motionless to the closing strains of the song. "Really, I didn't."

A burst of applause exploded from the crowd, and everyone began to drift back to their own business. Everyone but Caron and Rick. He still had a grip on her waist and had no intention of letting go.

"I bet you trample 'em in court in those heels," he eventually muttered, his eyes slits under the brim of his hat.

Caron raised her eyes from the mat of dense black hair sprouting from his open-necked shirt. "I'm proud of my performance. Though my show doesn't compare with yours, cowboy."

"You could do just as well with the right partner," he proposed silkily in her ear. "I'll come dance on your turf sometime soon and prove it. We'll really give a jury something to deliberate."

Caron peeled his hands from her body with urgency. "You will always be a wise ass."

"You came back for more."

"Maybe I'm a customer."

"Maybe I'm not sellin' any," he growled back in surprise.

"The customer's always right."

He pushed up the brim of his hat, drawing his face to hers. "The customer got the brush yesterday."

"Still too slick, Rick."

"Still too mouthy, Caron."

"I know about that baby, you oversexed rebel," she ground out.

Rick drew short. "You think I'm too sexy?"

"I think you're just plain too much!" she shot back in exasperation.

A high-pitched squall pierced the air all of a sudden, paralyzing them both. A teenage girl with frizzy blond hair, dressed in a hot pink jumpsuit, shuffled forward with a carrot-topped bundle squirming in her arms. "Hey, Rick, you didn't say anything about fixing leaks."

"Give him to me, Hayley," Rick directed in resignation, opening his arms to receive the fussy child. He set him in the crook of his arm to examine the large wet spot darkening the inside leg of his blue-and-white striped suit. "Ask the hired help to do you a favor . . ." He nuzzled his mustache into the baby's tear-stained cheek, favoring the teen with a disgruntled look.

Hayley shrugged. "Sorry, man. Pay me a plumber's wage and I'll fix all the leaks you want."

"Get back to your broom." Setting his hat on her head, he shooed her off.

Caron favored him with a smug look. "I saw you holding him in the window last night."

"Guess the jig's up, Bobber," he surrendered with a sigh. "Caught by a peeping Tom."

"Short for Robert?" Caron quizzed in hope.

"Short for Thomas, I'd say."

"You're impossible!"

"Your nose is too short now," he complained. "I want you to know that, Caron."

"Oh, for Pete's sake!" she lamented, throwing her hands in the air. "Listen to me, Rick. This baby changes everything. He's the best little offer I've got right now."

Rick stared at her for a long, calculating moment. "Let's settle this in the back. While I change the Bobber."

The storeroom was piled high with crates of detergent and fabric softener. A workbench and a weight bench dominated the back wall near an old wooden staircase, which Caron guessed led to Rick's overhead apartment. A freestanding sink was on the left, and beside it a worn changing table piled high with rattles and disposable diapers. Rick shut the door behind them, muffling some of the noise. "Hold onto him while I run upstairs for another suit," he directed suddenly.

Before Caron could protest, Rick thrust the fussy bundle of flesh into her arms. She handled the baby awkwardly, attempting to brace his back with one hand, pushing his head against her lapel with the other. Already uncomfortable and ornery, he sensed her inexperience and let out a yowl. "Now, now, Bobber. Do you want the world to know that I'm at a loss with miniatures like you?" She pressed her lips against his temple, finding his wispy head of red hair soft and mildly fragrant. Under calmer circumstances, holding him might be a treasured moment, a chance to learn the finer points of the task. As it was, he writhed and kicked with all his might, preferring to lunge into the unknown rather than tolerate her.

"Tormenting another generation of males, I see," Rick mocked upon his return. With easy movements he set the whimpering baby on the table and peeled off his wet clothing.

Caron paced around the cramped room. Just like the front, this stock area was cluttered. "You know, if you put things in order, worked out some sort of system, you'd have a lot more space to move about. It would really increase your efficiency."

"As it happens, I believe things here are extremely efficient," Rick countered. "I make a good profit. My customers are delighted with the atmosphere. In short, I am a rousing success. This rebel soared beyond the neighborhood's expectations and made good. On my own terms," he added with emphasis.

"That's the only way you could ever do it," Caron relented.

"Being inventive has given me a lot of satisfaction," he boasted eagerly. "There are thousands of orderly Laundromats all over the country that follow your expectations. But this place is more than just a place to wash clothes. It's a second home to a lot of nice people. We watch all the big games on my wide screen television. We have pool tournaments. We even have the occasional karaoke contest."

"Don't forget your dances," Caron added wryly. "With each and every new babe."

"It's all in fun," Rick said. "Get me one of those wipes from the blue box on the windowsill."

Caron peeled a moist cloth out of the plastic container and brought it to the changing table. "Rick, I can't help but wonder if you're carrying this king-of-the-neighborhood thing too far. No matter how noble the gesture, hiding an infant from his relatives without cause can land you in deep trouble."

"I never said Bobber was the Ramsey baby," he cautioned. "File that fact away in your orderly noggin." He folded the soaked diaper in two and handed that to her. "And file this in the basket over there, please."

Caron reluctantly obliged, stopping to wash her hands at the sink. "So, where is his mother?"

Rick shrugged, swabbing the Bobber's behind. "She, ah, had to get away for a while. Needed time to regroup."

"Because the love of her life died," Caron swiftly speculated.

He turned to her with a flick of annoyance. "I never said the mother was in love with James Ramsey."

"Oh, you're as slippery as ever!"

"And you're still marching to your own conservative drummer," he accused reaching for a fresh diaper. "Still trying to fit in with people who don't know squat about the real joys."

Caron wandered over to finger the baby's eiderdown curls. "You've never had to concern yourself with fitting in, have you? You always managed to slide along as the big man, dazzling them with your charm. I've had to work harder for my place."

"I doubt it," he differed mildly. "What do you think a rebel does once the diplomas are handed out and the spotlight dims?"

"I wouldn't know," Caron promptly admitted. "I went on to school with a full scholarship and worked my tail off."

"I took the less scenic route and climbed up off the street," Rick assured, busily clothing the baby with fresh things. "My journey was a little different, Caron, but I've been knocked around by life like everyone else. I too have the customary dues statement stamped paid in full—for this decade, anyhow." He turned to regard her with a forthright expression. "How can we ever reach a compromise in this jam we're in? One minute in my arms and you step on my foot."

Caron closed her eyes briefly to veil her uncertainty. How could she tell him she tripped because being in his proximity still turned her to Jell-O? That grazing his body had left her a stumbling, bumbling idiot? She wanted to be the alluring one this time!

"Your feelings for me are shading your sense," he accused.

Though the statement was true, Rick had no concept of her feelings for him. Never had. And much to her own bewilderment, Hotshot was one subject she couldn't pin down in definitive terms. He cluttered her heart and her mind in much the same way junk cluttered his shop. No rhyme, no reason. No cure.

"Caron, we are down to the wire here. Your own detectives will find out about me soon. You're either with me all the way, or out there with them."

Caron stared mutely at the thumb he was tilting toward the street. The thought of being left out of his world devastated her. She already knew it to be the coldest, loneliest place on earth. She raised her thumb and finger an inch apart. "Give me something, Rick," she requested in a small voice. "Something to convince me that we won't land up in federal prison on kidnapping charges."

"I happen to be carrying out James Ramsey's last wishes," he confessed, raw emotion fanning lines around his eyes. "At least I'm trying to. You see, James began to regret telling his Aunt Agatha about the baby. He knew if she spilled the beans to Douglas, there would be inquiries. He didn't want his child to deal with the old man if it just wasn't right. Get it?"

"Why you, Rick?" she asked, struggling to understand this complicated man's sense of loyalty.

"James and I were close," he said softly, cuddling the baby possessively. "He was a beloved member of this tight-knit family neighborhood."

"It's such an awesome responsibility!" Caron exclaimed, trying to ignore the tug at her heart as Rick planted a kiss on Bobber's head. To be loved so thoroughly by Rick must be heaven on earth. "You are at the helm of the heir's destiny for cryin' out loud."

Rick's jaw settled into a grumpy line. "That's the way James wanted it, I tell you. Is it so hard to believe that he could entrust me with such an important task?"

It was! And she knew it was written all over her face.

"I was hoping you'd take my word for it, help me on faith. But that obviously isn't meant to be." Rick gave her the baby once again and withdrew his wallet from his back pocket.

Caron drew a heart-pounding breath, causing the sober baby to glare up at her suspiciously. Did he have the Ramsey medal in there?

But it was a folded sheet of paper he extracted from the credit card holder. "It just so happens that James put his wishes in writing. I guess he sensed the end was near, that he might never see me again." Rick blinked long black lashes. "He didn't."

Caron traded the baby for the paper. Unfolding it under his scrutiny made her feel like a heel. She couldn't lower her eyes to the page.

"C'mon, read it, satisfy your doubts." When she continued to focus on him, he growled in anger. "Let me start you out. 'Dear Rick . . .'" Caron's gaze dropped to the letter as Rick began to recite it word for word.

It is with sincere affection that I write this note of goodbye. It is up to you to decide upon the inheritance. I would have done so myself, had I been stronger at the end. You, young man, must be my strength. Check out my stonehhearted father, Douglas. If he doesn't meet your standards, back off! I trust you to do what's best.

Love, James

"He even signed it with love, Caron. This is family. This is commitment."

Caron refolded the letter and carefully stuffed it in his shirt pocket, giving Bobber's bottom an awkward pat. "It's so hard for me to improvise. . . ." She trailed off under his strained features, again searching for words that wouldn't hurt him any further.

"I respect your standards, Caron," he said quietly, swaying in place to soothe the baby.

"You most certainly do not!" she cried in awe.

"Okay, I don't," he confessed, with the pout of a boy caught playing hooky. "I think you're being difficult when you could be easy, just like always. At least you gotta admit I've shown you some good faith here. I've laid out a big-time ace, shared with you an extremely personal note that no one else will ever see. Still you hesitate!"

"If I could just talk to the mother. Maybe she has the proper heirloom. That would seal up the doubts for everyone."

Rick pinched her lips closed with his fingers. "Leave her out of this for now, okay? James asked me to set it right."

Caron pushed his hand away. She wanted to be fair. And she certainly had the right claim. The letter proved it beyond a doubt. If only she could let her guard down with Rick. But she knew better than to risk her heart with the Hotshot.

"You should understand James's doubts about Ramsey," he continued on. "You know the old guy is pretty crusty at times."

"I guess I could give you one chance at him," she relented wearily. "I'm invited to a party at his place Saturday night. He said I should bring an escort."

"That shindig reported in the papers?" he asked in delight. "Sounds perfect!"

"I'll pick you up around seven-fifteen," she told him, turning on her heel to leave.

"Yes! My record's complete!"

She whirled back in fury to find him twirling Bobber in the air like a pudgy, squeaky, red-nosed missile. "What do you mean?"

"You are the last girl in the class of '83 to officially date the Hotshot," he teased. "All eighty-one are now accounted for."

"What bunk!" Caron scoffed suspiciously.

"I swear it's true," Rick insisted with an indolent shrug.

"Take my roommate, Megan Gage, for instance," she quickly challenged.

"I did." Rick's grin was infuriating as he turned the baby in his arms to face her. "Tell her to go home and ask, Bobber."

"Eat dirt, Wyatt!"

"See ya Saturday, Quick Draw."

Caron marched full tilt through the front and out the door, nearly colliding with Judy Bernside on the sidewalk outside. The elder woman's arms were full of folded blankets.

"Let me help you," Caron offered breathlessly as the stack began to tumble.

"Thanks, dear. I'm parked right over here." Mrs. Bernside circled a burgundy sedan, opening the back door on the driver's side. She proceeded to stack the blankets on the seat, two at a time.

"Looks like you're sprucing up the bedding," Caron observed.

"Rick's large capacity machines sure come in handy during my fall and spring cleaning sprees," she explained, closing the door with a satisfied thud. "So nice to see you again, Caron," she said, digging her car keys out of her purse. She paused and scrutinized Caron with a sigh. "I still can't get over it. You looking so striking. Your mother must be proud...."

"In her own way perhaps," Caron replied with a wan smile.

Judy Bernside nodded in understanding. "You were one of Sharon's nicest friends back in school. I knew you'd do well."

"I suppose you're wondering what I'm doing here today," Caron ventured.

"Doing at a Laundromat with no laundry?" Judy's blue eyes lit up merrily, her voice betraying her curiosity. "Rick does get a lot of visitors from your class. It's sort of a watering hole for those old pals who wish to keep in touch." Her tongue clicked as she realized her blunder.

Caron made light of it with a laugh. "I never was part of that crowd. Rick and I were sparring partners, nothing more. I was here today—" She checked herself in midsentence, realizing she could no longer tell this woman everything with teenage impulsiveness. "Actually, Rick has a legal matter that needs attention."

"Well, he couldn't be in more capable hands, I'm sure," she said, squeezing Caron's hand. "Did him good to face a woman who didn't melt in his arms."

"That dance gimmick must get him a lot of mileage," Caron wagered.

"Mmm, yes. All in all, it is a positive thing. So many people like the romantic nonsense of it all. Still," she said with a smirk, "it was a lark to see no swoon in your step."

Caron bit her lip. No simple swoon for her. She'd clumsily plunged into his arms with a painful stomp!

"Well, don't let him give you a run for that retainer," Judy advised in farewell.

"I won't," Caron promised warmly. "The baby certainly is cute," she ventured casually.

"Bob? Bobby?" Judy laughed. "Doll baby, that one."

"He belong to a neighbor?"

Judy paused in thought. "Why, I don't know. It's just like Rick to help out someone in need, though. He's as generous as the day is long. Mind you, he still has that smooth, wily streak in him. Just as always. Some of the old biddies round here think he's reborn, that it was their stern attention years ago that turned him around." She hooted at the idea. "Rick's parents raised him and the three others just fine without any interference. Sure they were a ragtag bunch of kids. Sort of spoiled perhaps because the mister and missus were so grateful to have adopted so many."

The Wyatt children were adopted? What an intriguing revelation. But what a practical explanation! Rick's own circumstance was most likely fueling his emotions concerning Bobber, driving him on to find the baby's rightful place. "I didn't realize Rick was adopted."

Judy nodded in understanding. "Hard to believe, considering how well they all blended. Most folks didn't know. The Wyatts moved in with the four of them already in tow. I suppose Eleanor was fearful her kids would be set apart from the others if the news leaked out. Of course it doesn't matter now that they're all grown. But Rick," she said, shifting gears, "he was a charmer from the word go. Nothing those ladies did or did not do fazed him any. It's wonderful that he's managed to polish his charm and funnel his skills into something useful."

"Still the same under the skin, however," Caron ventured in judgment.

"Yes, that's just the way it is," she agreed with a jingle of her keys. "Once a hotshot, always a hotshot."

5

"LIFT THAT LEG just a little higher. Let it pull just a bit farther than last time...."

Caron groaned in unison with the other leotard-clad women lying on the exercise-room floor at the Ladies Only Fitness Club. Along with Megan, she was a regular on Thursday nights from six-thirty to eight-thirty.

With a fresh law degree and a grinding determination to be a lean, mean litigator, Caron had enrolled in the club's complete program of diet and exercise. And how it had worked! Since then this workout of aerobics and calisthenics had become a religious ritual, a spiritual as well as a physical exercise. The heart pumped and the soul vented. The most noble of quests for personal caretaking.

So why in the world was she thinking of Rick Wyatt with every hip roll, every leg lift? All of their differences slid to the background as she invited his sexy image into her mental comfort zone. He was luring her to carnal thoughts with his flashing dark eyes and luscious-looking mouth. It was as if he were right there. Almost.

She moved her right leg up and down, trying to kick the fantasy away to the beat of a popular Janet Jackson song. But the ploy didn't work. The more she kicked, the clearer he became, stretched out before her, face-to-face on the floor.

Eventually she abandoned the battle. With lids hooded to shield her naughty thoughts, she indulged in some personal exercise erotica, allowing Rick to possess her every pore. To claim her like a man on fire. Soon she was aflame, lost in her own imagination.

The music eventually stopped with shattering abruptness, leaving her alone and untouched. Caron snapped her eyes open and ankles shut at the same moment, scanning her fellow huffers for any reaction. It was a ridiculous feeling, suspecting that someone might be privy to her private pleasures. No one could read her mind.

Jennifer, the group's lanky blond leader, bounced to her feet at the mirrored wall up front, motioning them all to follow suit. "Great job, ladies. Especially you, Caron," she marveled. "You really got into the workout. It helps to let yourself go. To give in so totally."

With a small self-conscious smile Caron shifted from one foot to another, pulling her creeping red leotard back over the curve of her bottom. If one only dared do it in real life.

As Jennifer rummaged through her box of cassettes, a tardy Megan Gage entered the room with a sheepish grin on her pert face. She paused at the bench against the side wall to peel off her jeans and sloppy sweatshirt down to the pink leotard and tights underneath. She skipped into her regular spot beside her roommate, fingering her head of mussy golden curls.

"I must look a fright," she gasped to Caron. "I ran over to Talbot Center to do some shopping this afternoon and lost track of the time. Did I miss anything?"

"It seems not," Caron retorted, simmering over Rick's claim to have once made it with this trusted friend.

Megan looked puzzled. "What's the matter with you? You lose your case today?"

"No, I won."

"Then it must be Rick," she rattled on, doing some quick arm stretches. "Did you confront him about the baby? Tell him you caught him in the window?"

"I did," Caron affirmed tightly. "And he told me something. About the two of you."

Megan froze, her face draining of color. "He told you about me?"

"Just a teaser," Caron uttered under her breath. "Maybe you could supply the details."

"I will," she promised defensively with a toss of her head. "Later."

Later couldn't come soon enough for Caron. When the roommates made their usual stop at the club's snack bar after class, the mood was far from festive. They sat stoically at one of the small round tables in the ice-cream parlor atmosphere, sipping on apple spice iced tea, glaring over the rims of their tall, cool glasses.

"Can't you see what you're doing to yourself, Caron?" Megan lamented. "You're falling into the same old pattern with Rick."

"Hey, I'm mad at you," Caron fired back. "Don't try to pull that exasperated buddy stuff on me."

Megan shook her head, keeping rein on the conversation. "I never would've encouraged you to check him out, had I known you'd crumble into a million pieces all over again. I thought it would be a lark for you to face the ghost of prom past, wallop him with your charms."

"I believe Rick may still have the same potent effect on me as chocolate fudge cake," Caron philosophized remorsefully. "Both have proven far easier to resist when separated from my senses."

Megan rolled her expressive blue eyes. "You and your penchant for sweets. For Rick." She fidgeted with her glass on the tabletop under Caron's expectant gaze. "What did Rick tell you about me?"

"He said he had you," Caron supplied, her anger flushing her cheeks.

"*Had* me!" Megan squealed, causing heads to turn. "In the historical saga sense?" she asked in a hush.

"Tell me about it, Megan," Caron ordered.

"Well, it was at the beginning of senior year," Megan reluctantly began. "We, ah, went to the mini golf course, then sorta made out in front of my house in his old Chevy. But believe me, Caron, we didn't get far. You know how my father was about my dating at that age. He had the yard light on within five minutes. The one we used for nighttime volleyball games," she clarified for impact.

"He claims he had every girl in the class except me," Caron flared in pain.

"He always did love to bring a gasp to your lips, didn't he?" Megan reasoned.

"But what a thing to say, if it isn't fact," Caron challenged in mortification.

"It sounds like a silly joke," Megan consoled, giving her hand a pat. "Face it, you are far more straightforward than the average person, far more precise. While it makes you a great attorney, it leaves you gnawing over some things that should be taken lightly. Many people indulge in teasing exaggeration just for fun. Rick is a master at it."

Caron's voice remained steeped in betrayal. "We've always shared everything as the closest of sisters would. I have no secrets from you, have I?"

"I intended to confess the next day," Megan claimed in good humor. "Boy, oh, boy, I couldn't wait to tell you. Figured I had the bet snagged."

Curiosity quelled some of Caron's anger. "Well, didn't you?"

"The snake never did officially call me on the telephone, before or afterward. I obviously eventually backed out of telling you. You were serving on the student council with him and so wound up about it all. . . . The whole thing seemed better off buried."

"I see," Caron conceded with effort.

"Really, Caron?" Megan asked hopefully.

Caron nodded with fervor. "I've been downright ridiculous."

"We've always been the truest of friends," Megan assured her. "No man has ever come between us. Not ever."

"There was that pianist at Sonny's Grill," Caron reminded her.

"So there was," Megan relented. "But we tickled his ivories when we caught on to his game!"

They sipped their tea between giggles.

"Caron, don't let Rick slide you into a vulnerable position," Megan advised hesitantly. "Not with your job at stake."

"He won't," she assured defiantly. "He can't."

"He still can," Megan differed softly. "You nearly cracked up when you thought he'd taken on every girl in class."

"It was silly of me to get so upset," she scoffed with a wave.

"So possessive," Megan countered with compassion. "He didn't understand the depth of your feelings for him the last time around, and I suspect he still doesn't."

Caron rubbed her temples with a sigh. "Don't tell me to back away, because I can't. Not only is he harboring a baby under suspicious circumstances, he's got a letter from James Ramsey, instructing him to act on behalf of the heir." Caron paused as Megan gasped. "He's insisted upon my discretion. And here I am, trapped into conducting useless interviews to shield him."

"Did he show you a medal?" Megan asked in a hush.

"No."

"Maybe he has the wrong baby, Caron."

Caron shook her head forcefully. "Oh, no. I recognized James's handwriting in the letter. I figure Rick doesn't trust me enough to cough the medal up yet. Figures he can always burn the note, return the baby to its mother, and claim it was all a mistake if he wants to. But if I see the medal, I can identify it for Douglas Ramsey. Rick could never escape then."

"You're considering turning him in?"

"Yes."

"So, what did you do in the end?" Megan demanded.

"I asked him on a date, of course!"

"Seriously, Caron."

Caron flushed in embarrassment. "Douglas Ramsey asked me to his bash on Saturday and I invited Rick along."

Megan's rich, husky laughter shook her tiny body. "Only you, Caron, could end up in this mess with Rick Wyatt. Just keep in mind that he really is a lot like chocolate to you—a sweet treat that goes straight to the hips. *Straight* to the hips."

"I NEVER THOUGHT I'D SEE this gorilla in a monkey suit ever again," Kyle Wyatt crowed, strolling into the storage room of Hotshots early Saturday evening.

"Just hoped to outshine you for once," Rick jeered, scanning Kyle's brown suit and striped tie. Kyle often toiled away weekends at his accounting firm, donning a suit nearly round-the-clock. Despite the fact that he almost lived in conservative attire, Rick could see him as nothing more than a gangly goof-off.

Rick was the indisputable lady-killer of the family, no matter what he wore. Tonight he was drop-dead chic, his broad-shouldered figure draped in an elegant black tuxedo with a crisp white shirt and crimson cummerbund. Seated in a battered swivel chair, his thick hair was being attended to by Hayley. The teenage Hotshots employee was not sparing the spray as she brushed his black coils back off his face to a thick ducktail cascade.

"So, when was your last formal affair, Ricky? Prom?" Kyle's question was rhetorical, the sort of dig an older brother takes at a sibling. A year younger than Kyle, Rick had always been the brunt of his brother's humor. Rick, in turn, retaliated by pestering his two little sisters, Angie and Erin, to distraction. The four of them were still on close terms, even though the girls had left the neighborhood to raise children of their own.

"Maybe if you shaved the overtime once in a while and put on a suit just for the fun of it, you'd snag a date for yourself," Rick suggested. "C-P-A meets G-A-L."

"According to the grapevine, it sounds as though you did some fancy steppin' to get this G-A-L," Kyle fired back. He watched Rick fumble with the black silk tie at his neck for a moment or two, then stepped up to the chair to slide it into a smooth bow.

"It's a little tight," Rick croaked playfully, stuffing a finger in the starched collar of his dress shirt.

"I don't doubt it," Kyle snorted. "Considering the size of your head."

"Hey, lay off the Hotshot," Hayley sniped as she spritzed and brushed with the flair of a temperamental artist. "He's on a mission."

"Yes, little lass, it was I who put Rick on to Caron Carlisle's connection with Sharp, Krandell and Peterson," Kyle smoothly accredited himself. He dropped into a wooden chair beside the changing table, stretching his long legs out on the concrete floor. With a small cowlick at the back of his sandy head and the mischievous twinkle in his hazel eyes, the twenty-nine-year-old looked more like an overgrown teenager than a businessman.

"Only a louse would've kept her bombshell looks a secret, though," Rick growled, spinning in the chair to confront his brother.

Kyle chuckled. "Hotshot on the hot seat. How sweet it is." He gazed at Rick's brooding expression with some surprise. "Hey, you aren't falling for her, are you?"

"Nothing so foolish," Rick denied, knowing better than to ever deliberately give his tormentor ammunition. His feelings for Caron at the moment were best described as ticklish—something big brother would have a field day with! Rick just didn't understand what Caron was trying to do to him. She was so flirtatious, then so guarded. So hot, then so cold. If she was responding to his behavior, he was lost, totally bewildered. Sometimes she seemed geared up in the present, and other times she would slip back to some fretful place in the past. Was she specifically disappointed in him? Was she stewing about their old duels?

"Yo, Ricky," Kyle broke in, snapping his fingers. "You sure Caron doesn't have you by the nose?"

"I'm just intrigued with the new shell on the old engine," he claimed evasively. With an angry squeal Hayley dashed his face with sticky spray.

"That's no way to talk about a girl!"

Rick winced in apology, wiping his sticky brows. "Forgot about you, kid. Sometimes you seem too young to know."

"Remember when you were sixteen, Rick," Kyle began. "Why—"

"Never mind," Rick cut in sharply, reaching out in an effort to cup Hayley's ears. She twisted away, not about to miss anything. "Just cut the chatter about my past, brother," he ordered, settling back in the chair.

Kyle raised his hands, pleading no contest. "Don't let me get you all riled up over Caron Carlisle."

"I am not riled!"

"He was like thunder when she was here the other day," Hayley reported. "Almost tossed her out."

Rick shot her a dirty look. "I am fine now. She's graciously giving me what I want. A chance to question Ramsey."

"And that's all you're after from that scrumptious creature." Kyle regarded him in doleful amusement.

"Considering the circumstances of James's last request and my duty to carry it out, I would think you'd ease up. I don't find it amusing either, that you kept her transformation from me. She put me on the spot!"

"I heard she was gorgeous," Kyle relented, raising his shoulders a fraction. "But you know I only listen to rumors for the vicarious pleasure of it. I leave the spreading of them to Ma."

"I owe you," Rick warned with a stabbing finger.

"With the tangled web you're weaving, you won't have time for me," Kyle predicted, stretching his arms above his head.

Hayley paused with brush in hand. "That web stuff is really deep, Kyle, ya know?"

"Ah, if you were a mite older, Hayley," he said with a sigh of resignation, "I'd—"

"Do her taxes," Rick cut in snidely.

Kyle sniffed in annoyance. "Ha, ha. If you seriously wanted to pump up my love life, you'd hook me up with Caron's roommate."

"Megan Gage?"

"I hear she's a nurse now," Kyle said. "I had a crush on her all the way through school."

Rick grinned. "I might do it. She and I were golfing buddies way back when...."

The jingle of the entrance bell echoed to the back.

"Since I'm officially on laundry duty tonight, I'll check it out," Kyle announced, popping out of his chair. He leaned his lanky body against the doorjamb, peering out front. "Evenin', Ma!"

Rick grinned from his chair with a knowing nod. Of course Eleanor Wyatt had to see him in his tuxedo. His parents still lived only three blocks from Fairfax in the family's green stucco rambler. She popped in often, to gossip with her friends and do an occasional load of laundry to support his business.

"Evenin', Mrs. Foley," Kyle called out in a second greeting, turning back to measure Rick's look of growing consternation.

"Evenin', Mrs. Monahan," Kyle greeted for a third round, nearly laughing out loud as Rick slapped a hand to his eyes. "Look who's here to see you off, Ricky," he reported with feigned guilelessness. "Ma. And Ma's dearest friends."

The terrible trio. At one time it had been the fearful foursome, when Caron's mother had been part of things. But between Deborah Carlisle's thirst for the big time, and the prom incident, the friendship had given way under the strain.

To Rick's relief only his mother breezed into the back room.

"Hi, Ma. How's the Bobber doing?"

"Papa's having the time of his life looking after him," Eleanor said, her round, wind-flushed face beaming. "Such a treasure."

"Sure you don't mind having him all night?" Rick asked.

"We expect you to share him," she chided, a trifle hurt.

"So, you just in the neighborhood, Ma?" Rick asked as she unbuttoned her gray cloth coat.

"I live here, remember?" she said defensively, busily tugging the knit gloves off her plump hands. She looked up suddenly, surprised to find Rick's chocolate eyes dancing in merriment. "Oh, you tease!"

"You're always welcome here, of course." Rick looked off into space, his angled jawline twitching. "What's your pleasure tonight? A quick game of pool? A little air hockey?"

"Such nonsense, Ricky!" she chided with the click of her tongue.

"You come to check me out in my threads, then?"

"Why, of course not," she scoffed. "Just came from supper at the new Chinese place, just passing by on the way to the movies."

"I see. How's the food over there?"

"Dandy and economical." She paused expectantly, then blurted out, "So stand up and let me get a look at you! You know the early show starts in fifteen minutes!"

Rick eased out of the stuffed vinyl chair. He patiently towered over the stout, gray-haired woman now circling him with the lint brush she'd slipped out of her purse. "So you were just passing by, huh?" he couldn't resist goading as she brushed at the immaculate fabric.

"I'm always out on Saturday night. Papa has his cards and I have the girls." Eventually satisfied that the lint was licked, she straightened up to face him with a clucking sigh. "Lean over, your tie is a mess."

Rick complied, grasping the lint brush thrust at him.

"Hey, I fixed that tie," Kyle objected.

She tossed her fair-haired son a look of pity. "No surprise to your mother." She turned back to Rick in earnest. "Now Ricky, be on your best tonight."

"I will shine," he promised magnanimously.

"Whatever they serve, you eat it."

"I will eat everything on my plate, Ma."

"Whatever you do, don't fight with that Mr. Ramsey."

"I will eat everything on my plate, Ma."

Eleanor Wyatt snapped the tie into a bow, glaring up at her son. "You could blow this whole thing with your attitude."

Rick drew a breath and turned to Hayley. "Go out front and hold down the fort, will ya?"

"Yeah, sure, boss," Hayley replied. With a pop of her gum, she was gone.

Rick turned back to address his mother. "I am determined to check out Douglas Ramsey to my satisfaction. Whatever it takes."

"Just don't antagonize him," she stubbornly persisted.

Rick's square jaw tightened. "If he was the warm fuzzy type, none of this would be necessary."

"Sometimes you have to work with people, like those ambassadors do."

"An ambassador I ain't," Rick snorted.

"Watch out or you may land on your rump," she cautioned.

"A place I've been many a time," he good-humoredly finished her thought. "Besides, I have Caron to pave the way if I go too far. She knows just what to say and how to say it."

"She didn't grow up hoity-toity like the mother, did she?" Without waiting for an answer, she forged on. "You know Deborah never thought much of the folks around here. Thought she was better even when she lived two blocks over from us. I'm telling you when the mister used to get the morning paper off his stoop, his pajamas were nothing special. Mrs. Hines saw him lots of times while walking her poodle."

He closed his eyes for a moment, images of Quick Draw's soft green eyes and gently curving mouth setting him aflame. "Caron's an angel, Ma. A livin', breathin' angel."

"Well, I heard she's prettier now...." she trailed off wistfully.

"Does everybody know that?" Rick demanded.

"I imagine so." Eleanor pried her brush from his clenched hand and stuffed it back in her purse. She proceeded to dig around in the roomy bag, ultimately extracting her wallet.

"Now, Ma—"

"Just settle down." She opened her wallet and fished a folded ten-dollar bill out from behind a photograph. "Can't have those Carlisles thinking you can't put on a fine date. Can't have it ending like the last time...."

"I don't want your money, Ma." Rick started a dancing dodge around the short, quickstepping woman who had tirelessly tried to keep rein on him during his childhood. "I'm going to the Ramsey mansion for Pete's sake! He's loaded."

"This is for a soda or something afterward. And Papa would say you should have it. Just call him up right now and ask him," she dared in time-worn persuasion. "Heaven knows you can't be walking around with a pocketful of coins from those machines out front," she reasoned, trying to stuff the bill into his breast pocket. "Your tuxedo trousers will sag from the weight. You'll be lopsided and Mr. Ramsey won't even talk to you."

"How many times have I told you, Ma, Rick doesn't spend all that change he makes," Kyle protested, grasping her arm with laughing eyes. "He has real bills of his own, just like you and me."

"Your little brother doesn't make the kind of money you earn at that fancy office," Eleanor scolded under her breath, tapping Kyle's hand away. "It's change."

"Rick is a successful entrepreneur," Kyle insisted, stopping short when he caught Rick's warning look. The brothers had traveled this territory before and Rick just didn't have the time tonight.

"Thanks for the dough, Ma," Rick pleaded no contest, leaving the folded bill in place behind his white handkerchief.

"So, hadn't you better get going?" Eleanor asked with a quick glance at her watch.

"What about your movie?" he queried.

"I've got another minute to see you off."

"I'm waiting for Caron," he confessed reluctantly. "She's picking me up."

Eleanor's ample bosom heaved in loving exasperation. "Is your pickup truck broken again, Ricky?"

"No, Ma, Caron insisted upon doing things this way. And she did invite me out. I didn't want to argue the point. I'm trying to win her over, remember? Minimize the bickering ways of our youth."

In response, Eleanor opened up her wallet again. "A little gas money is in order. Papa would say so."

"Cut this out, Ma!" Rick closed her wallet and returned it to her purse. "The money, the tux, none of it is going to mellow me out!" He zippered the sack and thrust it back into her arms. "I am what I am!"

"A rebel through and through," she relented in exasperation. "Always trying to prove yourself. Why, even as a toddler, you'd draw a chalk line for the mailman to cross. He had to do it to reach our mailbox, but you made such a production out of it, pretending he was a bully primed for a rumble."

"Why bring that up now?" he grilled impatiently.

"Because I want you to acknowledge that you still have an attitude beneath all this razzle-dazzle," Eleanor replied, not the least bit put off by the stormy expression on his handsome face. "You could spoil this opportunity."

"My customers love me," he insisted, angry that any female could slip beneath his skin, even the one who knew him best.

Eleanor wagged a chiding finger at him. "You still draw invisible chalk lines each and every day! You're about to slouch your way into Ramsey's fancy place with a chip on your shoulder."

Rick held firm under her unrelenting gaze. "Well, James had faith in me, didn't he? And it's all falling into place. The coincidence of having Caron positioned at the law firm just gives me the feeling that it'll be all right."

Eleanor raised a brow in speculation. "How much have you told Caron?"

"Just enough to satisfy her." Rick drew air through his teeth, trying to control his racing pulse. The thought of really satisfying Caron was sending lightning bolts of desire through him. She was so hot now, with her sophisticated air and streamlined body. But so damn controlled. What a confining prison for such a burnin' babe!

If only . . . He had no idea what it would be like to be on her side on any issue. Still, making his cause her cause just seemed like the ultimate strategy. The unattainable dream of yesterday rekindled in the form of this heir business.

Caron was still intellectually out of his reach, but irresistible just the same. The last thing he'd expected to feel was the familiar sexual pull. But the pure chemistry that had fueled their verbal duels in school still lingered between them after all these years. A cruel trick of nature, but undeniably true. The flame had flared as cleanly as a match struck to sandpaper. He couldn't stop thinking of her in that little yellow hat. Dressed in nothing but the teeny tiny hat.

"Careful, son," Eleanor was rambling on. "Caron's a shrewd one."

He smiled wanly. "Hopefully not as shrewd as you, Ma."

"At least not on the subject of you, let's pray."

Hayley popped her frizzy blond head into the room. "There's an old man out on the sidewalk in a uniform, Rick. He's driving a limo and looking for a guy dressed posh enough to ride in one."

Eleanor raised a hand to her heart. "Those Carlisles have really made the big time!"

"Not that big, Ma," Rick scoffed, glancing in the small mirror on the wall on his way to the door.

"Then she sent it on purpose, just to show us up," Eleanor assumed in affront.

Rick raised a dubious brow. "Caron?"

"*Deborah*, you sweet, ignorant child!" Eleanor brushed her sons aside and marched through the place to join her friends at the huge window facing the street.

Rick trailed after her with Kyle at his heels. "Good night, Ma," he said, planting a kiss on the top of her head.

"He is parked right at the bus stop!" Eleanor cried, jabbing an accusatory finger. "The seven-twenty will be here anytime now. Then Deborah will get a ticket!" Her prediction sent a ripple of laughter through the group of window peepers. "We'll see who has the clout around here."

"Hold her back, Kyle," Rick instructed under his breath as their mother touched the zipper of her purse with an itchy trigger finger. "I feel an extra limo allowance coming on."

Sure enough, she and Kyle were soon tangling with the purse.

Eleanor raised her head to deliver a parting shot as Rick darted for the door. "Whatever you do, Ricky, don't let that girl stuff anything down your cummerbund again!"

He touched his forehead in a small salute. "Don't worry, Ma. Every thread's insured this time."

6

RICK CLIMBED INTO the plush interior of the limousine to find Caron perched on the rear bench, a delicate red rose on a bed of gray velvet. He swooped down beside her, cozily grazing her thigh with his trouser leg. His gabardine against her sateen scraped noisily in the hushed vastness of the enormous vehicle, causing them mutual pause, bringing home memories of prom night. Together again in the very same colors. In the very same electrified state of mind.

Rick gazed deeply into her gem green eyes, wondering just what she was thinking, wondering if he should say something, anything about the aura of déjà vu. He decided against it for the time being. He couldn't afford to lose his cool. Checking out Ramsey with a clear head was crucial.

"This is one hell of a back seat," he remarked abruptly in boyish wonder, shifting his interest to the massive automobile. "Not cramped like my old green Chevy. Remember that car I had in school, Quick Draw?"

"Yes, of course," she replied. "Have you ever stopped to think about how many people have never once sat in the back seat of their own cars?"

"Do you realize how many hot-blooded teenagers have?" he challenged with a good-natured wink.

"Perhaps you would've been well served with this sort of divider," she proposed, gesturing to a sheet of tinted glass separating them from the front seat. "I'm sure, given the chance, the neighborhood mothers would've purchased one for your Chevy. And the fathers would've gladly installed it for you."

Rick's eyes grew warm and guileless. "Think it would've stopped me?"

"It is bulletproof and soundproof. Yet . . ." She trailed off with heavy doubt in her tone.

Rick slanted her a knowing look. "Sounds as though this isn't your first ride."

She gasped in disbelief. "In a back seat?"

"In here, dope!"

"No, as a matter of fact, it isn't," Caron replied with a trace of pride. "Mr. Ramsey often provides me with luxury transportation. I can tell you it soon spoils a person."

Rick lifted a lofty brow. "Well, if this is a blatant ploy to lure Bobber to your side with a taste of the good life, you're wasting your time."

Caron slanted him a wary look. "He's not corruptible?"

"He's not home."

Caron couldn't help but laugh. "Perhaps I'll swing by again tomorrow. If he hasn't flown the coop permanently, that is."

Her querying statement brought a wry curl to his mouth. "Bobber won't be disappearing just yet. My folks have him for an overnight visit is all. I'll tell him you were asking after him."

Caron frowned in confusion. "Why, wasn't that your mother at the window?"

"Yeah. Pa's got sole custody for a few hours. At this very minute he's probably holding both Bobber and an inside straight close to the chest with glee." A tender note deepened Rick's voice as he reported his family affairs.

"Eleanor looked a bit disturbed," Caron openly fretted, raising a hand to her chin-length fluff of auburn hair.

Rick realized with pleasant surprise that it was a nervous gesture, for her glossy strands were styled as deliberately as his own. She was one tempting package top to bottom in her rose-shaded dress with spaghetti straps and filmy matching shawl, her exposed shoulders and legs now lusciously lean beneath satin-smooth skin. Knowing she still had a tender underside beneath the new look, that she still cared about his mother on any level, warmed him like a camp fire.

"Don't worry about Ma," he placated with a twinkle in his eye. "She's just a trifle disturbed over your wheels."

Caron's carefully made-up face grew stricken. "Surely she doesn't think I rolled through my old neighborhood in this monstrosity to rub the good life in your faces!"

He shook his head. "Naw."

Her sigh of relief was audible. "That's good."

"She thinks your mother sent you through the neighborhood in this monstrosity to rub the good life in our faces."

"Mr. Ramsey insisted upon sending it," she defended herself.

"I figured as much, Caron," he comforted, reaching over to catch her hand in his. Bypassing the sexy little thighs pressed together beneath the creeping hem of her dress took an enormous surge of willpower. But he couldn't take the chance of misreading her signals. If he made a move and she shoved him aside, he'd die, just as sure as if he lay down in the street in front of this moving limo. Losing her the last time had almost done him in. And he'd had youth and resiliency on his side.

Well, he'd grown up, clearing away a lot of that adolescent confusion. It was time to settle down, have a pack of kids. Rick wasn't sure if Caron wanted the works: the vine-covered cottage, the babies, the clutter those things brought into life. She certainly wasn't comfortable handling the Bobber. She was a tigress while fighting for the heir on principle, but the hands-on handling of a real live baby seemed to scare her. Of course that could be cured if it was just inexperience. If it was preference, that would be a major obstacle.

No matter what her preferences, Rick was currently head-over-heels in love with her all over again. He wanted to edge in closer, find out if it was possible to stake his claim and make it stick. But her behavior was too erratic. If she said no, the bouncing back would be impossible. The old heart just didn't hold the same buoyancy it had ten years ago.

"Did you explain it to your mother?" Caron broke in anxiously.

"No—"

"Damn you, Hotshot!" she cried, snatching her hand from his.

"I didn't have time, Quick Draw. The seven-twenty bus was due any second and Ramsey's man—"

"Franklin," Caron supplied.

"Franklin was in the loading zone."

"Oh," she said with pause. "Well, I imagine he doesn't deal with such restrictions very often."

"Don't worry about a thing. I'll tell Ma tomorrow that your mother didn't hire this stretch to yank her chain."

"Thanks." The snap in her reply was diminished by the fleeting softness in her eyes. She averted her gaze as he turned on her with unabashed curiosity.

"It's always been your nature to care for people," Rick pointed out gently. "I'm glad some things weren't altered along with your nose."

"Are you knocking my snoot or my mother's snooty attitude?" she wondered guardedly.

"Maybe both. Each seems a little too perfect."

"Mother really let some of her old cronies have it years back with her determination to make it in the big time—whatever that may be," she conceded wistfully. "I imagine your mom wasn't too thrilled with the idea of our reunion, no matter how businesslike."

"Their feud is their problem," Rick objected. "Our fathers never even entered into it!"

"Oh, yes, our duels are separate from the rest," Caron acquiesced without hesitation. "But our silly prom night clash did finally give them an incident to pin all of their silly differences on. An excuse to part company for good."

"Food fight is what they still call it in the neighborhood," he differed with a flash of white teeth.

Caron's small jaw dropped. "They still talk about it?"

"Yeah. Probably because no one's topped it. And this new date has fanned the old fires. Ma got to reminiscing about your hands in my cummerbund—"

"I hope you quelled her fears," Caron huffed, flushing in the dim light.

"Better yet, I got insurance on this number," he reported proudly, patting his lapels.

"You didn't!"

"Mr. Linden wouldn't let me leave the formal-wear shop without it," he claimed under her mortified look. "Not after he heard on the grapevine that I was tangling with you again."

"You spilled punch on me first!" she attempted to reason. "They all should remember that!"

"They do. Guess it's part of the reason they think we're a combustible combination. Face it, baby, together we're TNT."

"Well, be sure to respect this dress," she advised saucily. "*She* picked it out again."

He reared back on the seat in surprise. "Still making choices for you?"

"Still trying," Caron huffed.

"You tell her about us?"

"I merely told her that the nice young man who called her about the class reunion was accompanying me to the party. She assumed it was Paul Drake, of course."

His mouth curled mockingly. "It's naughty to lie."

"Advice from the master to the apprentice!" she accused. "Paul Drake indeed. What if she'd recognized the name?"

"There must be a few in the phone book," he reasoned calmly. "Besides, I consider the character an alter ego, so that minimizes the untruthfulness of it."

Caron offered no dispute. "I appreciated the easy out in this case. I believe you deserve a chance at Douglas Ramsey and it has nothing to do with her whatsoever. Though I don't like subterfuge of any kind, the less I tell Deborah the better."

"Sorry you didn't have the sort of childhood I had," he returned in understanding intimacy. "But I've always suspected Deborah loves you in her own way. Taught you how to fight for what you want, anyhow."

Caron's smile turned briefly brittle. "Yes, weaponry and strategy are her strengths. Her weakness lies in choosing the worthwhile battles. Money and position are her ideal, the gateway to happiness."

"Pretty sad, really," Rick said quietly.

"Pathetic!" Caron promptly chimed in. "And isn't Douglas Ramsey the prime example of shallow wealth? He's lived his life in an emotional limbo, focused only on getting to the top of the heap. Now, in the twilight of his years, he's realized what's been missing—the human factor. Despite his desire to change, he doesn't seem to know how to handle relationships. Happiness is an internal affair within each of us."

"So, you gotta boyfriend?"

"What kind of a question is that?"

"Can't blame me for being a little curious," he said easily, picking up on the dismay in her tone. "You were invited to this fancy ball, Cinderella, complete with the coach, the slippers and the flashy dress. Seems you had everything lined up but the prince."

"Mr. Ramsey asked me at the last minute, if you must know." In a motion of self-preservation, she pulled her thin shawl over her breasts. The filmy fabric only increased her appeal, drawing an enticing curtain of mystery over the mounds of soft flesh pushed up at her sweetheart neckline.

If he didn't know her so very well, he'd have sworn she'd done it purposely. But she hadn't. Her defensive shield was genuine. It was so Quick Draw.

"I don't have a steady, either," he confessed simply, making the obvious assumption on her status.

"Oh, you still think you know it all," she fumed, gazing out of the smoky window at the city lights.

"Give me a break! No guy in his right mind would set you free to roam the night in a billionaire's limo. Especially not with the Hotshot in the back seat. Fully insured till noon tomorrow."

Caron's face sheeted in astonishment. "Is that an invitation of some kind?"

"It's just a fact. Do with it as you will."

As each considered the possibilities, the car rolled along the highway like a magic carpet, heading for the outskirts of Denver. Eventually they approached the massive electronic gate built into the stone wall surrounding the Ramsey property. When they wound their way through the well-kept grounds spotted with mighty oaks and shrubbery, Caron reached over to the side seat and collected her black woolen coat and small black purse.

"Caron, why did you bring a coat if you're not going to wear it?" he wondered in bewilderment.

"I don't want to get mushed beforehand, that's why," she answered distractedly, gazing past him as they rolled to a stop under the massive stone arch at the entrance of the house.

Rick hid a smile behind his sleeve, totally convinced that Caron had absolutely no idea of just how lethally gorgeous she was tonight. He knew she'd been deliberately vamping him all week, but she was obviously unaware of her profound effect on him, naive as to just how much he wanted to plunge deep inside her. She didn't believe she had that sort of power over the male species in general. After all these years, she was still unsure of her beauty.

It was nothing short of a crime.

Crimebuster Rick to the rescue—if and when she found herself ready and willing to mush that spectacular dress.

A uniformed doorman was on hand to promptly open the door and assist them. Rick bypassed his arm with a fluid motion, stepping aside so that Caron could take the man's arm. Once her feet were firmly on the walkway, Rick took over as her escort.

The people milling at the entrance to the huge stone home turned to stare down the broad staircase at the unknown couple, most likely to see if they were celebrities. Rick enjoyed the attention, even if he and Caron lacked the proper notoriety. He'd never looked better or had better company on his arm. With an assuring pat in the region between her fanny and waist, he ushered her up the bank of steps.

"So, what do they do at this sort of bash?" Rick queried under his breath. "Dance, eat, play parlor games?"

"This sort of bash can be described as a high-priced schmooze session," Caron replied frankly. "People mingle, brag, and make connections both business and social. An orchestra will supply the music, which few will probably dance to. Buffet tables of food will be set out. Drinks will be served by uniformed help. Empty glasses will be whisked away promptly and efficiently."

"Faster than you can say baby bobber buggy bumpers?"

Caron's groan was audible as they joined the crowd streaming inside. "I imagine it's something like your Laundromat, but on a much bigger scale. Without the pool table and detergent.

"Good evening, Mr. Ramsey." Caron greeted their host warmly in the huge, crowded foyer moments later. He'd swiftly dismissed the trio of men he'd been speaking with at the sight of Caron.

"So pleased you could make it," he said with delight, his eyes bright behind his thick, wire-rimmed glasses.

She drew Rick forward. "This is the man I was telling you about this morning, sir. Richard Wyatt."

"I've looked forward to meeting you all day," Ramsey said, shrewdly surveying Rick as he pumped his hand.

"The feeling is mutual," Rick returned smoothly, meeting his gaze directly.

Ramsey's brows rose to a bushy V, his booming voice expressing a measure of bemusement. "So you are a classmate of Caron's. It's certainly a coincidence, you having contact with my late son and my attorney."

"Yes, Caron and I have been grand old friends since childhood." He smiled guilelessly. "Served on the student council together, that sort of thing."

"I was in the middle of a crisis at my anchor store in Boulder when her call came through," Ramsey reported without apology. "Naturally I didn't have much time to confer with her."

No time to discuss his late son's friend? Rick didn't care for the sound of it. But he could feel Caron's shoulder nudging his arm in warning. He decided to take heed for the moment.

"What did you actually say, Caron?" Ramsey paused in recollection. "That James patronized Mr. Wyatt's Laundromat?"

"Yes," Caron affirmed. "And he—"

"Odd stroke of fate," Ramsey mused.

"We marveled over the coincidence, didn't we, hon?" Rick wrapped a possessive arm around her shoulders. It felt so good to hold her, even if her body stiffened at his touch. She was undoubtedly bristling because he was setting a false precedence of their current "friendship." One chance and he would make it real enough.

"We marveled all right." Caron's response was bright, but delivered through clenched teeth.

"Caron and I have always been big debaters," Rick forged on, rubbing his hand down the length of her back. "Talk over everything. As it happens, we were discussing your article in the newspaper. I told her I happened to know James, that he lived not far from my shop."

"So you know nothing of a baby?"

"Not a thing," Rick confirmed without hesitation. "Was Caron right in assuming you'd care to meet with me anyhow?"

"Of course I'm glad she thought of bringing you," Ramsey said, his voice thick with emotion. "I—I'm sure you have many things to share, Richard." He took a cursory glance around the busy room. "Let's find some privacy for a nice chat, shall we?"

"My friends call me Rick," he told Ramsey in invitation a short time later as Ramsey beckoned them into a room in the back of the house. The trio had marched through a maze of corridors in silence, their feet pounding carpets, tiles and hardwood along the way. Ramsey turned on the wall switch and shut the heavy door after them with a thud.

"Why, look, Caron. Mr. Ramsey has a pool table after all," Rick swiftly noted with approval, his eyes sweeping through the oak-paneled room. "I have one at my Laundromat, you see," he revealed under the perplexed look of his billionaire host. "Though mine is a little less ornate," he added, stepping up to admire the table of carved teak.

"So you enjoy billiards, eh?" Ramsey's large face lit up over the prospect.

"Oh, yes, sir," Rick affirmed, wandering over to the rack of sticks on the wall. "We call it pool over on my turf."

"When the table's teak and the balls are ivory, it's billiards," Douglas Ramsey heartily maintained. "Brandies all around?" When he received double nods of acceptance, Ramsey headed for the bar in the back corner. "Yes, we play games here at the big house too, Caron," he said conversationally.

"I was attempting to draw comparisons between your party and one of Rick's gatherings at his Laundromat," Caron responded as she slipped into a butter-soft leather chair. "Hotshots is kind of a local hot spot."

"You see, I have to have most of my fun at work," Rick explained. "The business keeps me very tied down. I have some hired help, but I'm pretty much on my own." He wandered over to the bar and took the two stout snifters offered him by his host. He served Caron chairside, leaning against the wall of polished panel behind her. "I'm a self-made man without much use for regulations and fancy trappings."

Was Rick trying to pick a fight? Caron wondered in awe. How on earth would challenging Ramsey's luxurious lifestyle serve Bobber's interests? She twisted around to frown at him warningly. He rewarded her with a trademark rebel scowl.

"We have the self-made image in common, Rick," Ramsey assured him without rancor. "But you already know that I am immersed in regulations and fancy trappings. Though the reputation I have around Denver, around the blasted world as a matter of fact, is a little harsh. I'm more than a hard-edged businessman who worships the dollar. I'm a human being who is searching for answers, just like everyone else."

"I've heard you referred to as an old goat," Rick confessed. "But I don't take much stock in rumors and innuendo. I believe only what I check out for myself."

"Old goat, eh?" Ramsey chuckled with genuine amusement. "Imagine that, Caron."

"I can't," she murmured, shifting on the smooth leather at the echo of her own words. This rebel had a death wish.

Ramsey lifted his snifter to his lips. "Your Laundromat sounds like a creative business venture. An interesting concept, taking the boredom out of a decidedly bleak chore. Seems I'm not the only one here who can turn a buck," he added graciously, further groundwork for an amiable chat.

"But my people are top priority," Rick shot back.

Ramsey scowled, but kept his tone even. "As you may have gathered from Caron and the papers, I'm still struggling with the personal side of my life. I'm trying to mend my ways with the people close to me, give my grandson what he deserves. This search is of monumental importance to me. The fact that you knew James is of monumental importance to me."

"Yes, maybe we do have some common ground," Rick said quietly. He set his glass on an end table beside Caron and sauntered back to the pool table. "Yes, sir. The toys may be fancier, but it's still the same game, isn't it?"

Ramsey hesitated only moments before nodding firmly. "Rack 'em up." He rounded the bar and joined Rick to select a stick off the rack, sparing Caron a brief look. "Caron, perhaps you'd like to go upstairs and look in on Agatha now. She's been anticipating your visit."

"Why, certainly." Caron recognized an order from a powerful client when she heard one. She drained her glass with great reluctance and set it on the table beside Rick's. She hadn't intended to leave them alone for a minute! Both on a probing mission. Both difficult men. Rick the rebel versus Douglas the goat.

"You'll find her private elevator at the end of the hall, m'dear," Ramsey directed, sizing up his stick. "It'll take you directly up to her suites. Her staff is expecting you."

Caron paused at the door. Rick turned suddenly, as if smelling her fear. He tossed her a cavalier wink behind the old boy's back. Would he have the good sense to temper his questions? He'd never shown restraint in his youth, even over the most mundane school issues. What would the grown-up rebel do, with a genuine cause to fight for this time?

Agatha Ramsey was indeed waiting for her. In the hallway with open arms. "Franklin called the moment you arrived at the gate!" she greeted, enveloping Caron in her frail arms.

Agatha was a tall, lithe woman, a font of timeless beauty and infinite knowledge—knowledge that unfortunately had to be challenged for accuracy on occasion. With teasing eyes and yellowed hair cut short and feathered around her small, delicate features, she couldn't be a more delightful companion for a lively chat. There was certainly no harm to her aimless reminiscences, as long as one wasn't conducting an investigation on the basis of her claims—as the law firm of Sharp, Krandell and Peterson happened to be doing. Caron hoped to continue their friendship long after the baby mystery was put to rest.

"We'll just have ourselves a little party in my parlor," she announced enthusiastically.

Caron followed the elderly woman into a cozy lamp-lit room filled with mismatched pieces of furniture and antiques, ranging from Art Nouveau to Italian Deco to Victorian.

"I thought perhaps you'd be downstairs tonight, Agatha."

"Oh, I could be," she asserted airily. "Douglas tells people I'm too frail to attend this or that." Her voice dropped to a conspiratorial octave. "Even that gruff old bulldog brother of mine doesn't have the guts to admit to his guests that I hate stuffy affairs, even at my stuffy age!

"I like my peace, my possessions," she rambled dreamily, gesturing for Caron to sit on a mahogany parlor sofa with sloping dolphin arms. "This room especially. It's off-limits to the staff. My personal maid is allowed in here once a week for light cleaning, under my supervision." She brushed her thin, veined hands together with glee. "Let's have a sherry, shall we, Carrie?"

"Let me serve you, Agatha," she proposed, half rising from her seat.

"No, I can still serve drinks." Agatha flitted off to a gilded walnut cabinet, which Caron guessed to be eighteenth century. "I hope you don't mind my calling you Carrie." She turned to Caron for approval, gripping the neck of a stout bottle of amber liquid in her fingers. "You've never told me if you like it."

"It's different, but I like it." Caron held her breath as Agatha splashed two sherry glasses full to the brim. Amazingly, she spilled not a drop.

"I had a close friend for many years named Carrie," she confided meditatively. "We modeled together all over the world, making our fortunes. She's gone now."

"Deceased?" Caron asked, taking the glass offered her.

Agatha plopped herself on the sofa beside Caron, taking a healthy gulp of wine. "No, just lost her mind is all. I hope my body stops ticking before my brain does."

"Me too," Caron agreed.

"You're such a pleasure," Agatha chirped. "I suppose you've come to talk about James again, and his baby. I'd like that."

"Mr. Ramsey shocked us all at the firm by advertising for the child," Caron intimated, twirling the stem of her glass in her fingers.

"I told him to tell you first," she was swift to clarify. "Though he's genuinely fond of you, dear, he does like to fancy himself in charge of everyone in sight." Her mouth lifted in what Caron recognized as her secret smile. "I was the one who came up with the idea of the medal hand-me-down, you know."

Caron stiffened. "What do you mean, Agatha?"

"Near the end, when James was fretting about Douglas and the baby, what to do about proof of parentage, I gave the medal to James to pass along to his son. Then, if the mother ever wished to enter the lion's den, she would have the entrance fee."

"Clever," Caron said.

Agatha tittered nearly to tears. "Just the right price, an appropriate entrée to the Ramsey dynasty. A simple silver dollar in a circular setting. It's a symbol of the first dollar Douglas cleared on his first department store fifty years ago. He wore it on a chain around his neck to the grand openings of Ramsey Department Stores for years and years. He was originally grumpy when he learned I nicked it and gave it to James." She paused for a breath. "But I was right to do so. Now he's grateful for the link to the child."

Caron's mouth curved fondly. "Mr. Ramsey didn't want any of us at the firm to know the precise specifications of the medal."

"But true, true friends share secrets," Agatha gushed with another sip of wine.

Caron gave her hand a brief squeeze. "Almost done with business," she promised. "Just how often did you see James during the years he lived on Fairfax Avenue?"

"Only occasionally," Agatha replied. "He'd never come here to the house, of course. Might run into his father. We'd meet in restaurants or galleries. You see, he shared my interest in art. Did I tell you that before?"

"No."

"Oh, yes, James had a gentility about him that roughshod Douglas never could have accepted." She paused with a wistful sigh. "I think James was better off keeping his distance from his father. They would've clashed constantly. James was a sensitive man, as was his mother. Had he lived, he never would've been equipped to run the Ramsey stores. It would've been nothing but sorrow."

It made sense. Only a sensitive man would've sent Rick on such a delicate mission, Caron mused. He'd obviously sensed Rick's own streetwise toughness and figured he was a worthy match for the old man. In this silent deliberation, she raised the sherry to her mouth. Her eyes widened as she realized the finely etched crystal in her hands did not have the same meticulous care given the glistening brandy snifters downstairs. A fine coat of dust lined the inside of the glass, partially dissolved at the wine line. Agatha really meant it when she said this room was left to her discretion! It was a wise reminder that this grand old lady had her frailties despite her bravado.

"You like the sherry, don't you, Carrie?" Agatha's hands fluttered fussily over Caron's hesitation and she drained her own glass in a final slurp.

"It's fine," Caron assured her. "I just had a drink downstairs and want to pace myself." She took one polite sip before setting it on the table before them. Oh, the things her own mother would be surprised to learn about the upper classes. Deborah had such an unvarnished image of how the rich folk lived, unaware that pain and tangled relationships plagued them along with everyone else.

"You had expressed interest in our family albums," Agatha ventured in open eagerness. "Would you like to see them now?"

"Very much so." As much as she wanted to trust Rick and his methods, she was determined to continue the investigation on her own, in a parallel, more detached manner. Rick was too fired up, too evasive to be trusted completely. A photograph of a Ramsey resembling the Bobber would be a valuable find. Something she could hold on to, even if Rick let go on his end.

"You'll find them in there," Agatha chirped, gesturing to a bookcase with beveled glass doors.

Caron retrieved the albums and brought them to the coffee table. "I'm looking for anything that could help me identify the baby if I see him," Caron explained, settling back on the settee with a book in her lap.

"Ah, identifying markings, eh?" Agatha nodded with a shrewd glint in her eye. "Have you had a lot of claims?"

"Too many," Caron replied dourly. "Some of them quite outlandish. Any solid leads would help tremendously."

"I'd like to see pictures of the babies," Agatha requested. "I believe I'd know a Ramsey if I saw one."

"I'll send over a batch for your perusal," she promised, impressed with Agatha's self-assurance and dedication. The knowledge that Bobber's photograph couldn't be included in the bunch stung her conscience a little, but the more she learned, the more she was sure James had good reason to put the heir's fate in Rick's hands. Agatha would understand her deception in the end.

Behaving so unconventionally was tough on Caron, so job jeopardizing as well! Rick certainly had honed his manipulating ways to perfection—crowding her into this jam! She wasn't sure which had a more profound effect on her, his verbal flimflam or his tantalizing touch. His massaging fingers on her shawled shoulders and bare back tonight right under Ramsey's nose came back to haunt her, titillate her; but most importantly, to warn her. A hand that could rock a cradle and her senses with the same deftness was one to be wary of!

An hour of thumbing through pages and pages of the Ramseys' pictorial history brought Caron no further clues. "I believe I'd better be joining my date downstairs," she announced, gauging the growing fatigue in Agatha's face.

"I would've enjoyed meeting your fellow," Agatha told her with a disappointed sniff.

"I'll bring him up one day soon," Caron promised as she returned the albums to their proper place in the case.

"We'll have a bit of a party then," Agatha rallied in merriment, flitting to Caron's side in slippered feet. "Just the three of us."

"I couldn't help noticing there are no professional modeling shots of you in the albums," Caron said with regret, arranging the books in the order she found them.

"Douglas didn't think it ladylike to include them in the family archives," she huffed. "Not many women worked and lived on their own in the old days, you know. As it is, my best work is on canvas." Agatha took several steps to the wall, drawing back a tapestry curtain. Rather than the expected window, there was an oil painting on display in a huge scalloped frame.

Caron drew an astonished breath. It was a portrait of Agatha. Circa 1920s by Caron's estimation, judging from Agatha's youthful face and figure and the silver-plated mesh purse in her hand. Save for the purse and a fox fur at her throat, she was totally in the nude. With masses and masses of the brightest red hair Caron had ever seen, tumbling over her ivory shoulders.

7

THE MOMENT CARON CLOSED the door to Douglas Ramsey's den, Rick turned back to the table to arrange the colorful striped and spotted balls in a pyramid on the green felt surface. "Eight ball okay, sir?"

"Fine. I know them all, Rick." Ramsey carefully chalked his cue. "I must warn you, I'm a serious player. I can concentrate on a business deal and the game with admirable dexterity."

"I'm good too," Rick flatly asserted. "I often whip someone's pants while washing someone else's."

"Your table get a lot of play?"

"Constant," he reported, skimming the lavish teak surface with covetous eyes. "Especially when kids are free to roam. You know, summer, after school, weekends."

"No child has ever touched this masterpiece," Ramsey confirmed the obvious.

"I like to lure the kids off the street," Rick explained, setting the white cue ball in position for the break. "They need something to do more than anything else. I know I always did."

"No experience with them, myself," Ramsey readily admitted. "You break. You're the guest."

Resting his stick in the crook of his thumb, Rick took careful aim at the cue ball. With a sharp crack it hit the triangle of colored balls, scattering them in all directions. The red one rolled into the left side pocket. "No experience, you say. But raring to jump into parenting with full force." Rick sized up his options while waiting for Ramsey's response. As important as the man's answer was, Rick was taking some pleasure in playing on the deluxe table, too. He could do absolutely anything while playing the game. Anything mental, anyway. With fluid grace he leaned over, poised his stick, and shot the cue ball into his blue one, sending it across the fine felt surface into a corner pocket.

By his expression, Ramsey appeared disgruntled by the questions and Rick's prowess in the game. "I'm willing to take the chance on the child."

Rick found Ramsey's autocratic outlook extremely irritating and took pleasure in sinking another ball. "Kids can't be returned like Ramsey Department Store merchandise," he informed him, pausing to chalk his cue.

"I know that!" Ramsey barked, his complexion reddening. "And maybe it won't be a successful union. But it's every man's right to know his grandson. If I step in now, while he's young, he'll accept me as a fact of life. Without his father's tainted opinion," he added with resolve.

"You gonna take total custody of him or what?"

Ramsey balked at his nerve. "Why do you ask?"

"Because I'm curious, I guess." Rick forced calmness into his demeanor, slightly shrugging his broad shoulders under his elegant jacket. "I imagine the entire state is curious. You opened the door when you put it in the papers. Frankly, I'm fascinated by you, sir. Because you're Caron's client. Because you're James's father."

"Yes, I thought we were going to discuss James," Ramsey complained.

"I didn't mean to offend you, sir. If you are uncomfortable with the issue of the heir himself—"

"I am not!" With large, weathered hands propped on the edge of the table, he leaned over with a glint in his eye. "I will tell you and anybody else this, young fella. If that child is living in a two-room apartment with an irresponsible mother, I'll take over in a wink. I'll sue for custody and make certain that boy has every advantage."

Rick bit his lip. Every advantage or every disadvantage? He couldn't debate Ramsey's negative effect on James's childhood, not without arousing the suspicion that he knew James much better than as a casual customer. That would get Ramsey fired up and digging around. The billionaire would trace the heir right to Hotshots in no time.

"I have many things to offer the baby," Ramsey continued as Rick bulleted his yellow ball into a corner pocket. "I want the kid to be happy. Your curiosity satisfied?"

"I wish you well in your hunt, sir." Rick raised his head from the table and flashed him a wide smile.

Ramsey shot him a wary look. "Just how well did you know my son?"

Rick held his gaze with a set jaw, quelling the emotions threatening to swallow him. "He was a regular customer."

"You engage in a lot of talk?"

"My place is a carnival of activity," Rick hedged, setting up his next shot. "People can come in for companionship, entertainment. I have the sports channel on my wide screen television. He sat in on a game now and then with the guys."

"James liked sports?"

Rick flashed him a pathetic smile. The old crust didn't even know that! Even with all of his recent probing! "Football, basketball. Seems he always wanted someone to toss a ball around with when he was a kid."

Ramsey nodded. "I was so busy when he was young. Then, before I knew it, he'd turned against me. The divorce split everything wide open and they both cut me off!" Ramsey growled. "His mother wouldn't take financial help. She felt that the money would become a bartering chip in our relationship. She wanted a clean break and got one."

Rick could read the frustration in the old man's eyes, the hunger to set the record straight with somebody. This was his chance to probe further. "Would this grandson ever see a game?" he asked quietly.

"Yes, yes, whatever he wanted." Ramsey paced the length of the table as Rick sank another ball. "You liked my son, didn't you?"

"Very much. I like most of my customers. All of my regulars."

"Is there anything you can tell me, Rick, anything that would help me out?" he asked, his forceful voice laced with desperation.

Rick shrugged uneasily in his tuxedo, uncomfortable in the clothing and the company. "I can tell you James was a good guy. If it makes you feel any better, I think he was satisfied with his life, with the decisions he made."

"Caron intimated that you were fairly close to him," Ramsey said unexpectedly.

"She did?" he asked mildly, concealing his annoyance. Caron had only spoken to Ramsey for a minute this morning and she'd managed to let that slip. Quick Draw was still true to her name.

"Did he have a special lady friend, someone he might have brought to your Laundromat?" Ramsey prodded.

"No, he washed his clothes all by himself, sir." Rick flared over the billionaire's glowering interrogation. His own mother certainly knew him well! But he couldn't stop himself. Like Ramsey, he would have to use intimidation in an effort to keep the upper hand.

"If he fathered a child, he must've mentioned it at some point," Ramsey snapped, his eyes turning hard. "Maybe during one of those male bonding sports broadcasts."

"All those games were, and still are, watched by a crowd of howling, backslapping, food-snacking guys intent on blowing off some steam and rooting for the home teams. No girls allowed, no babies allowed." Rick went about the business of sinking the rest of his balls with precision, taking the game without giving Ramsey one shot.

Ramsey leveled a beefy finger at him. "If you're hoodwinking me about the baby, I'm going to find out."

"What would my motive be?" Rick asked.

"I don't know," Ramsey bellowed bitterly. "Maybe you're after the reward. Maybe you thought I'd give you something just because you knew James."

"I don't want your money, man!"

Ramsey grunted. "It's difficult to believe you came here in an altruistic gesture!"

"That's your loss, sir. Not everyone is trying to jump aboard your gravy train." Rick's comeback was a quiet counterpoint to the old man's blast. But Rick realized it was too late to smooth talk his way back into the old man's good graces. If only he'd kept his cool from the start. Breezed in and out of this place without hassle. But in his zeal he'd been as demanding as Ramsey himself. Digging into his emotional well for the questions instead of his cache of common sense. If Ramsey sensed the depth of his feeling for James, he'd soon be digging into everything. And there was nothing he could do to stop him.

Well, all things considered, the trouble he'd taken to get inside the big house had not been wasted. This guy was one lousy grandpa candidate. Few questions remained in his mind at this point. What Rick would do when he ultimately got caught in his charade, and how he was going to hang onto Caron's job for her, however, were both on the top of the list. Though she was an honest woman, he was going to have to convince her to lie, say she had no idea what he'd been up to. And that was a half truth in itself. She had gotten him in here on false pretenses, but she really didn't know what was going on. He'd make the law firm understand if he had to.

"It's obvious you don't appreciate my visit, after all," he eventually muttered.

"I'm not accustomed to back talk from youngsters like you," Ramsey told him, his blunt nose reddening from equal doses of brandy and aggravation.

"Perhaps because they are employees in fear of unemployment," Rick shot back in anger. "I've avoided such groveling predicaments by building my own little empire. Where I come from, respect grows out of proving your stamina and grit. And showing some heart," he couldn't resist adding.

Ramsey sputtered for a response. "Why are you so angry? I should be mad over this skunking. I play to win. Always."

Winning at any cost. Rick received the message loud and clear. Grandpa of the year! "Thank you for the game, sir," Rick said, replacing his stick in the rack.

"I didn't have a chance here at all," Ramsey blustered. "Not in the game, not in this conversation. You came with a chip on your shoulder, didn't you?" When Rick didn't deny it, he sighed heavily. "Perhaps it's because I'm rich and James was not. Perhaps you just wanted to see what was denied him."

"There's many kinds of rich, Mr. Ramsey," Rick protested, eyeing the edge of his mother's ten-dollar bill in his breast pocket behind his handkerchief. "James had enough to get by. So do I."

Ramsey released a bushel of air from his large chest. "Well, then explain to me how we ended up in a squabble," he invited, "if you don't want my money and you're not fighting a battle for my late son."

Rick shoved his hands into the pockets of his baggy trousers and rocked on his heels. "There's a logical explanation, sir, one I know Caron would back up in a minute."

"YOU TOLD MY BILLIONAIRE client that you're a hotshot?" Caron gaped at Rick across the table in the bustling restaurant. "He wondered why you're argumentative and insolent, and your answer was that it's simply your nature?"

Rick nodded, rather humbled by Caron's scolding. The Ramsey party was two hours behind them and they were seated in the new Chinese restaurant near his Laundromat, polishing off lemon chicken and fried rice. He'd successfully dodged the subject of the pool game until now, by claiming that memories of James had welled up inside and he needed quiet time to deal with it. Certainly the truth as far as it went. He'd also sensed it would be easier to tell her here on his turf, where the walls were paneled with pressed wood and water came straight from the faucet.

"So, will I be getting an angry call tomorrow?" she asked, pulling the cloth napkin from her lap to dab her mouth.

"Depends whether he's a tattletale or not. Besides, it's Sunday. A day of rest for all of us hopefully."

"Douglas Ramsey's stores are open on the seventh day," Caron assured him dryly. "Isn't your place?"

"Not very often," Rick replied. He smiled in half-hearted hope. "Maybe he'll leave me alone. Eventually give up the hunt."

Caron shook her head. "I don't intend to second-guess him, not after his announcement to the press."

"Yeah, the old guy is a loose cannon all right," Rick grumbled.

"How could you let it go so wrong, Rick, after you worked so hard to get there?" Caron chided in confusion.

He leveled his fork at her. "It was your fault!"

Caron, sipping water from her glass, nearly spouted like a fountain at the accusation. "Me?"

"You went and told him that I was close to James."

"What should I have said?"

"That I knew *of* James," Rick scolded. "That he was just a customer."

"Douglas Ramsey wouldn't have left his guests for a private chat about his son's laundry," Caron sputtered.

"Well, he had a game plan of his own. Wanted to ask me all the questions. The nerve of the guy! Insinuating that I had ulterior motives."

"The inevitable is starting to happen," Caron cautioned. "He's grasping at any straw. And there's more," she added sympathetically. "I discovered tonight that Agatha had red hair in her youth. One look at Bobber and they're going to go bonkers."

"We'll see," he said quietly, pushing aside his half-empty plate.

"Oh, Rick," she confided in a rush, "I'm so disappointed that we didn't have a happy ending tonight. I had hoped that you and Mr. Ramsey would come to terms. That you'd have felt comfortable telling him about the baby."

Rick smiled indulgently over her romantic notion. "He has a problem with control, Caron. And I have a problem with his problem."

"There's always tomorrow," she said on an upbeat note.

Not with Ramsey there wasn't. But he didn't have the heart to tell her. "I'm still working on tonight," he protested good-humoredly, tossing some bills on top of the check. "Don't forget, I left my jokemeister brother Kyle in charge of my livelihood."

Her lilting laughter was refreshing. "Oh, that's right. Shall we go see if he's done any damage to that sudsy pickup joint of yours?"

They strolled leisurely down the sidewalk past the dimly lit storefronts, loosely holding hands. It was after midnight and the street was nearly deserted, save for an intermittent pedestrian or headlight beam. They stopped in front of the Laundromat, and Rick fished his keys out of his pocket. He opened the door, then ushered her inside the dimly lit place.

"First we must neutralize," he announced.

"You sound like a captain out of 'Star Trek,'" she teased.

"Just a shopkeep with an alarm system." He opened a gray box above the light switch and punched in the proper code on the numbered buttons. "Safe and secure."

"In your universe," Caron finished neatly.

Rick paused to lock the door once more, then scanned the room with a nod of satisfaction. "Yep, it looks like everything is in order."

Caron wandered around, a trifle lost in the obscurity of the dark, deserted room and in the confines of her own uncertain heart. "Kyle help out often?" she ventured in conversation. "Somehow I can't imagine him tinkering with all the gadgets in here."

Rick broke into an easy grin. "He doesn't have a mechanical bone in his body. I shudder to think of what would happen if a hose burst or a machine shorted while he was in command."

"Figures still his specialty?"

Rick thrust his hands into his pockets, leaning a shoulder into the pop machine. "Juggling numbers and eating junk food by the pound remain his passions. Though he'd like to include a certain little nurse in that buffoon act of his. . . ." he trailed off.

Caron blinked in surprise. "Megan?"

"Yeah, it seems he's always admired her from afar. Wants me to fix him up."

"Really?"

"Just told me so tonight."

Caron's breathing quavered as she stood near the row of dryers, recalling her last late-night visit. The place held the same intimate ambiance, with the single bulb glowing over the door, the machines gleaming white in the shadows. She fingered the collar of her black woolen coat, wondering where this uneasy moment was going to lead.

Rick passed her by, reaching over the dryers to tilt the wooden blinds shut against the front pane. Caron's eyes traveled with him, a quiver racing the length of her body. The air around him was heavy with tension and detergent, and a recently consumed pizza. She had never wanted a man so badly. Never wanted so desperately to be touched. Even if it meant there was no tomorrow attached to the proposition.

"What are you thinking about, Caron?" he asked as he fussed at the windows.

Caron stared longingly at his back. "Just that, by golly, you got through the night without spilling a thing on me."

"So, what are my chances?" he asked huskily, spinning on his heel to confront her with the most raw expression she'd ever seen on a man.

Her heart leaped up to her throat, making speech nearly impossible. "What did you say?"

"Does it seem right to fix Kyle up with Megan? I have to be sure of success, you see. Can't set up my own brother for a fall."

"I think it would be a chance worth taking," she murmured, her face warming to a pink over her misunderstanding of his intent. "It just so happens my people are important to me, too. I wouldn't want anybody to end up with a broken heart."

"She sure was an attractive little gal," Rick went on, fumbling for conversation. "Lots of fun, too."

"Yes, she confirmed your date," Caron said crossly.

Rick wondered suddenly if Caron could be feeling territorial about him. What a titillating thought! "I just meant that Kyle would probably do well by looking her up," he sought to explain.

Caron's eyes never left him as she drew open her coat and placed her hands on her hips.

Rick quaked with desire as he drank in the heaving breasts spilling out of her neckline, the way her fingers pressed into her curves, pulling her dress taut over her belly. Was it a deliberate ploy? "Why, Caron Carlisle, I swear you are trying to seduce me every time I come into range."

"Not every time!" she cried in affront.

"You were the first time."

"Which first time?"

"The most recent first time." He moved in closer.

Caron nearly melted as he caught her chin in his finger again. "I just want you to see that I'm attractive, Rick."

"Of course you are!" He dipped his mouth to hers hungrily.

Caron absorbed the impact of his crushing kiss, of his powerful body crowding her back against the dryers. He'd held her by the chin only the briefest moment this time, proceeding to use both hands to strip her coat away. Soon he was caressing her with at least a hundred fingers in a thousand places. But something troubled her. The white enamel surface of the dryer was shockingly hot, heating her bottom right through the fabric of her dress.

"It's burning," she squeaked urgently.

"Yeah, baby," he growled against her lips.

"I mean the dryer."

With a moan of reluctance, Rick pulled his mouth from hers and reached around her to set his palm on machine number four.

"Is it an electrical short in the wiring or something?" she wondered in panic, her fingers curled around his lapels.

If this interruption had been instigated by a woman other than Quick Draw, he'd have seriously doubted her true and genuine interest in making love. Considering her penchant for prudence, however, his doubts about her were only marginal. Caron simply worried about the practical things by nature. A most cautious babe always. But somehow he had to figure out just where he stood with her.

More than anything in the world Rick wanted Caron to want him. But he had to know for sure before she sent him over the edge.

"Can't you see that the sparks flying from me right now are far more dangerous than any old machine could be?" he demanded incredulously.

"But what does it mean, Rick?"

"Only that Kyle was treating his number friends from the office to some highjinx laundry service," he soothed with a crooked grin. "He can really make this place rock with a pocketful of change." There was a moment of silence between them, Caron staring up into his eyes, hands still clutching his lapels.

"You still make 'em rock, Hotshot?"

The question was soft, full of a quiet desperation. This was it! The final reassurance he'd been longing for, the necessary benediction.

"You bet I still rock," he drawled, fingering the shimmery shawl knotted at her chest. He removed the delicate strip of fabric with care, drawing it across the length of her shoulders, grazing her bare skin with its stiffness. She shivered openly over the small erotic gesture.

"Last time . . ." Her voice trailed off fearfully, back into the distant past.

Rick grasped her trembling hands in his. "The last time was just an adolescent appetizer which has left me starving, Caron. Think you can handle this hungry man, back for more after a ten-year fast?"

8

CARON COULDN'T BELIEVE her ears. He'd been pining for her for the last decade? It didn't make any sense. He'd unceremoniously dumped her after they'd made love in his Chevy on prom night—on the very seat covers she'd sewn for him! The one and only time they'd really ever been intimate after the kissing games of their childhood and he let her drop out of his hands forever. To this day the class of '83 didn't know that the couple's fiery encounter at the dance had led to the ultimate adult act. Her sharp mother had instantly figured it out upon her arrival home, in a different car, her dress and hairdo in a state. That was the real reason for the rift between her and Mrs. Wyatt. Caron was sure no one else knew other than Megan. After all, Rick immediately chose to make it past history by not returning for her the following day as promised. Just another conquest for him.

What on earth was Rick trying to do to her now, insinuating they should pick up right where they left off? On so many levels she wanted to do just that! Every nerve ending in her body was alive, crackling in electric anticipation. But some sort of explanation was in order. He'd said a lot of things the first time round and she'd blindly believed in him, without her characteristic reserve. Could she afford another one-night stand with the only guy she'd ever really loved, just for the sheer physical pleasure of it?

"You all right?" he asked.

"Very all right," she murmured, winding her arms around his neck. She would not think about the last letdown. He wanted her and that was all she needed for the night.

With a ravenous growl he sucked at the hollow of her throat, leaving a wet trail of kisses along her creamy shoulders. She tilted back as he nuzzled his face in the peaks of her uplifted breasts, delving his tongue down between the cushy mounds. Heat spiraled down her spine along with her zipper as Rick opened her dress with a single fluid tug. The spaghetti straps were no anchor for the small, gaping garment. It ended up a crimson heap at her feet.

Rick's eyes grew slitted and predatory as he moved back a step to absorb the erotic goddess of his dreams—all grown up in a strapless bra, garter-belted stockings and high-heeled shoes.

Her supreme primitive fantasy was unfolding before her eyes. Rick's stiffened body was nearly vibrating over his concupiscence for the new her. He seemed primed to swallow her whole.

The darkness of the room and the headiness of their carnal reunion gave her the courage to play the vamp of his dreams. She nudged the toe of her shoe up his trouser leg and spoke in sultry tones new to her tongue. "I've never stood before a tuxedoed gentleman like this before. Natty down to the bow tie."

"I'm not feeling like much of a gentleman," he murmured, chuckling without apology, his hand eagerly stealing to his throat.

"Let me start you off." She shimmied closer.

"You did this last time, too," he recalled huskily.

Caron's fingers stiffened at his starched collar as vivid memories of their youthful sexual encounter swept over her like a tidal wave, making her once more feel like a plump, insecure virgin. "You still remember it all?" she asked bleakly, frozen in time, in spirit.

"I remember everything," he revealed proudly. "Women are flattered when a man remembers, right?" he asked, puzzled over her sudden distress.

"I was hoping that once you saw the new me, you'd forget the other time," she confessed, avoiding his eyes as she loosened his tie and unbuttoned his collar.

"Forget one of the most precious moments of my life?" His voice was thick with shock as he gently kneaded her arm.

"You don't mean that!" she snapped angrily, wrenching free. "Not any more than you meant forever back then. Look," she placated, blinking back the tears. "I understand now why teenage boys whisper promises in dark cars to get what they want. But you have no right to continue to pretend you meant the things you said back then. It certainly won't make me more receptive now. That chubby kid with only her wits to feed from, still lives deep within my heart, Rick. I can accept starting anew. Good grief, I can hardly keep my hands off you—the chemistry is still that strong. But don't pretend you cared before. I won't let you."

A mask of hurt pulled his features tight. "I've always cared in my own way, Caron," he assured. "You've never been less than a real beauty to me."

"Not true!" she cried out. "You would've settled for me from the start. Returned my love!"

"You *loved me?*"

"Oh, shut up!" she squealed, pushing at his chest. "Of course I did! And how do you think I felt way, way back when you kissed the daylights out of me for a whole summer, then went on to all the other girls? How do you think

I felt when I toiled three years for the student council presidency only to have you zoom in and snatch it away? You couldn't leave me alone, Rick. You just had to keep stepping on my heart until it was crushed flat."

Rick shook his head in mystification, as if trying to translate her words to another language. "Caron, you must try and understand. Your beauty was never an issue. It was there, it was natural. It was a joyful sight to a hot-blooded kid." She tried to protest, but he pressed his fingers to her lips. "I simply could not handle your smarts. The older we got, the more evident it became that your wit far surpassed mine. I liked the limelight, being on top, and it killed me to accept that you had the brains to best me. You didn't drive me away. My own fears of being second-best did."

Caron felt chilly, standing before him in next to nothing, feeling chubby even though she was not. He must have sensed her inhibitions, for he drew her against the solid expanse of his chest.

"Oh baby, I was trying to prove myself a man with all of those girls. Teenage boys do that. But I joined the council to get your sole attention, prove I could survive on your turf. I was too dense to figure out why it made you mad. I thought you'd admire me for it. And you did seem to enjoy our verbal battles. . . ."

"I've been fighting my whole adult life to be the sort of woman men find attractive," she quavered. "I never wanted to feel like a rejected little girl again."

"There was never anything wrong with you." He raised his thumbs to the twin teardrops rolling down her hollow cheeks. "Your shape was just a little curvy. I loved it! I even loved your old bumpy nose."

"You don't deserve all the blame. I was an insecure mess even without you," Caron admitted with a sniff. "My mother raised me to believe I could never be perfect enough for the right man, and she keeps reiterating the fact in her own little ways."

"She's doing you a grave injustice," Rick agreed.

"But so did you, you know," she told him brokenly, making an admission she swore she would never make. "You built up my esteem, my hopes, that night you made love to me. Then you took it all away when you didn't show up the next day—as you promised you would!"

Rick splayed his hands across her bare back, finding it so, so silky. "Caron, we have to talk about that particular morning-after. And we will—soon," he hastily vowed under her belligerent look. "But we must choose a time when we're calm, understand? This is a charged-up moment for us already. All this other stuff, it's getting in the way of—for lack of a better word—the climax of our evening. It's up to you to decide if we stop here or if we—" he grinned rakishly "—go on ahead."

Caron noted that his hands were moving along her gartered bottom now, trying to sway her decision with skin-tingling persuasion. "I can't back off now, Rick," she moaned heavily. "Tonight is all that matters for us. Your eyes are still as addictive to me as a barrel of Hershey's syrup. I just want to dive in and wallow all night long."

The admission jarred him. "But what I mean is—"

"Don't bother with the pillow talk."

"Caron!"

She knew she was unraveling before his eyes. Her long, thin fingers moved over his face, skimming inside the curve of his ears. Her eyes roamed his fully clothed body with serious intent.

"Caron, I don't know what sort of man you think I am," he said incredulously. "But I want you to know that I do have an explanation to offer. I want you to enjoy our lovemaking with that understanding. I want you to have a little more blind faith in me."

"I don't know what to believe right now," she confessed on an impatient wail. "You've asked for so much of my unquestioning trust as it is."

Rick shut his eyes for a brief moment. "I know. I can't help it."

"I just know sex has never seemed more right," she coaxed. "Let's go for the best, outdo the last time."

"Caron, I don't know if we can do it any better than the last time," he entreated in earnest, his hands gliding along the slope of her hips.

Her eyes darted up to his, nonplussed by the admission. He meant it.

"Let's just build up a slow steam and let things escalate naturally," he suggested huskily. "We'll build on our sweet adolescent encounter, let it enhance our adult passions...."

"Let's just forget," she pleaded.

"Let's remember," he insisted, pressing her fingers to his mouth. "You took off my tux then. Do it again, Caron."

The slight pressure of Caron's delicate hands working the buttons on his stiff white shirt caused Rick to shudder openly. His pleasure gave Caron incentive to forge on, pushing his jacket over his shoulders. "You needn't be so cautious," he murmured. "I'm insured, remember?"

Caron laughed in comic relief, eagerly peeling him bare, layer by layer. Standing before her in nude magnificence, Rick took her very breath away. She sank her fingers into the forest of black hair on his chest, moaning. "Where are we going to do this, Rick?"

"Why, the hottest spot in the place," he said, slapping a palm on the dryers.

"On top?"

"Yep."

"Won't it be awkward?"

He grinned boyishly. "I don't know. It'll be an experiment for both of us." Rick dug into his jacket pocket for change and stuffed the coins into several of the dryers clear down to number seven. He set the timers and they hummed to life, tumbling hollowly with heat.

Knowing that Rick had never done this with any other woman gave Caron a feeling of comfort and lunacy at the same time. "Maybe I should take off my things before we—"

"Don't touch that stuff!" he cautioned. "It stays, it's mine."

"Even the shoes?"

"Especially the shoes," he growled, pinching her chin. "I too have several fantasies yet unfulfilled. Have had them since you leaned against number seven in your little yellow hat."

Caron wove her arms around Rick's neck as he drew her close to his sinewy length. His shaft grazed her lacy garter belt once, twice, undulating for entry to the nylon barrier housing her femininity. Clasping his lean buttocks in her long fingers, she picked up his rhythm, lavishing in the burning friction they were creating.

With a sudden sweep she was in his arms, gently deposited on the humming beds of warm steel. Her heels clanked against the top of number four as she stretched out on her back.

Rick stood over her in the shadows, feasting upon her reclining form with hungry eyes. Ever so gently he skimmed the inner bow of her thigh with the tips of his fingers, along her stocking, then over the top to her exposed skin. With a sharp breath he slipped underneath the garter belt crushing her nest of curls. When she groaned in satisfaction, he lifted her leg, drawing it over his shoulder. Caron shuddered in open delight as his touch invaded her tender moist folds, exploring, searing her sensitive nerve endings. Eyes glazed and gleaming in the dimness, he weaved his magic on her, unabashedly watching his own moves and her responses. Heat seared up through her abdomen, a red-hot coil about to spring into flames. A clenched hand on his thick, muscled arm, she soon reached climactic heights.

Rick eased her leg down, climbing atop the machinery in one leap to hold her quaking, shuddering body. "Oh, how I love you," he moaned into her hair.

"Don't say it, Rick," she choked out in huffs, clamping her shaky hands on his rock-solid shoulders.

"I mean it and will say it." Rick pushed himself to a prone position, his features stormy with ache. "Having you back again. It's all I ever wanted. It's never been as sweet with anyone else."

"Just believe in the moment, Rick." Caron licked the circle of her lips, inviting him for a taste. "I'm your baby tonight."

Rick's mouth was on hers with relish. Caron invaded his mouth with her tongue, savoring the taste of him, the same bittersweet taste of the first time.

"I want you inside of me, Rick," she cajoled huskily.

"I've waited so long—" He broke off, choked with a labored passion.

Caron drew him down, arching her back into the solid warmth of his body, fusing it with hers. His hair-dusted legs rubbing into hers caused delicious sensations to shimmer clear through her stockings. She wound her legs around his waist, her high-heeled shoes grazing his back. "Shall I take them off now?"

"No!" His order was a ragged utterance as he poised overhead for one last look into her sweet face. When her legs nudged into his waist, he plunged inside her with an urgent thrust. He drove into her over and over again to the tune of her enticing urgings, soaring on the mounting thunder in his ears. When her cries grew reedy with need, he exploded inside her.

With a moan of victory, Rick lightly collapsed on her length. They huffed together in a sweat-slicked heap for a long while. "We topped the first time," he rumbled deeply. "Who'd have thought it possible?"

Caron placed her hand on his rapidly beating heart. "It all seems like a dream. A dream I don't want to awaken from."

"Then you shall spend the night up at my place," Rick proposed, tweaking her nose. "When you awaken, you'll know it's real."

Caron struggled to sit up, her stockings and garter belt askew. "Do you think that's proper?"

Rick regarded her wickedly. Propriety hardly seemed an issue worth debating in that outfit of hers. "I know that I don't have enough coins to spend the night on these blasted dryers," he teased.

"What does that bed of yours run on?" she asked.

Rick rolled off the machines, hoisting her over his shoulder. "I rock that one without so much as a nickel!"

THE FRONT DOOR BUZZER of Rick's apartment sounded at eight o'clock the next morning.

"Where's that coming from?" Caron asked sleepily from the kitchen doorway.

Rick, standing at the coffeemaker near the fridge dressed only in a pair of baggy gray sweatpants, spun around at the sound of her voice. Picking up twin mugs of steaming coffee from the counter, he paused to leisurely peruse the tossed-over kitten rubbing her sleep-heavy eyes. "Guess we really mushed that dress of yours, didn't we?" he asked in gentle teasing.

Caron cast a look over at the rosy garment hanging in wrinkles on her form. "I'll cover it with my coat," she decided in the throes of a yawn.

Rick delivered a mug to her at the doorjamb where she was nesting, impulsively kissing her cheek. He didn't have the heart to tell her about the detergent stain. He'd discovered it a half hour earlier when he'd gone down to retrieve their clothing from the Laundromat floor. Must've happened when he backed her up against the dryers. He'd wrecked another fancy dress. Wait till Deborah found out!

The buzzer sounded off again, as sharp as the sun slanting through the square window above the sink. Oh, how he hated this interlude to end! Pretty soon the whole world was going to close in on him, and he just might lose Caron because of it. He needed more time alone with her. More time to join them at the hip with Krazy Glue bonding. As it was, her faith in him was shaky at best. She wanted to believe in his convictions and was doing quite well with the ones she understood. But the big quake hadn't hit them yet. Rick wanted to have the sturdiest foundation possible when it did.

One thing was certain. He would never let her go again. They'd reconnected last night as if there hadn't been any lapse in their relationship. And once he explained about the first time, she would give it a prized spot in her memory, savor it in the manner it deserved.

"Rick, the door," Caron prodded.

"It's just reality calling us back," he conceded regretfully into her short cloud of mussed hair.

"Might be too important to ignore," she reasoned.

"Don't worry." He inhaled one last gulp of her fragrance before pulling back. "No one's ever backed off from me without a fight." Rick set his coffee on the counter and headed across the living room to the door. His mother, in the company of the Bobber, was on the other side.

"What on earth, Ricky," she chided, bustling past him. Rick stepped out of her path as the bulky diaper bag slung over her shoulder bumped his rib cage. "I was beginning to think you were still spinning around in Deborah's limousine." She thrust the cheery baby into his arms. "I think you should go put on a shirt. No one ever knows who may be calling—" She stopped.

"Caron's calling at the moment, Ma," he said, adding a necessary look of warning to the needless announcement.

"You did it again, didn't you, Rick!" Her loud, sudden lament caused Bobber's face to crumple against Rick's bare chest.

"Ma, we are consenting adults," Rick stated, nuzzling his bristly chin into the baby's bright red hair.

"Together one night," she scolded in awe. "And you did it again!"

"Mrs. Wyatt, please—" Caron interceded, jolted awake by all the commotion.

"Shame on the two of you for doing this to me!" Eleanor dumped the diaper bag and her purse on the kitchen table.

"Ma!"

"Just look at her dress, Richard Wyatt," Eleanor challenged with a jabbing finger. "Deborah will expect us to pay for it again. I will refuse this time too, I tell you!"

"My mother will not charge you a cent," Caron objected, openly suppressing a smile.

"Did she purchase it, Caron?" Eleanor demanded, standing her ground on the kitchen linoleum, a short, round thundercloud in her gray coat, a white scarf tied under her chin.

"Yes, she did," Caron admitted. "But—"

"You two children deserve each other!" Mrs. Wyatt threw her hands into the air.

"You are absolutely right, Ma." Rick moved up behind his mother with a stricken-looking baby in his arm. "Now tell Bobber you didn't mean to yell."

Eleanor gently patted the baby's cheek. "Don't you dare grow up like this rebel, baby boy."

"Ma, don't brainwash the Bobber."

"I should've known something was afoot when I couldn't get you on the phone," she clucked. "Then to be roused by Douglas Ramsey!" She shook her head in disgust.

"Mr. Ramsey called you?" Rick asked sharply.

"He said he got no answer at your Laundromat last night or this morning. Caron's roommate gave him your home number and he claims it's been busy for hours."

"That persistent old—"

"Goat?" Caron supplied glumly.

"Exactly!" Rick agreed.

"Look over here," Eleanor huffed, stomping to the shelf holding the telephone. "The receiver is off the hook."

"Incredible," Rick mocked, puckering as Bobber fingered his mustache.

"So it's no accident, then." Eleanor replaced the receiver with a thump. "So, you did manage to antagonize that rich man out of his senses."

"He certainly did," Caron affirmed in disapproval.

"No wonder you're incognito," his mother scolded. "Hiding out to lick your wounds after defeat. What would the neighborhood kids think of their hero?"

"They'd think I was a fallible human being," Rick ground out fiercely. "Wrung through the spin cycle by the Ramsey family disaster. I tried to be kind, to make my points politely, but the old guy wouldn't have it."

"And now he's no doubt turning the tables, checking up on you." Eleanor sized up her son with an insightful eye. "Ricky, you're in too deep. As much as I liked James, he wouldn't want this to take its toll on you."

Rick prowled the room with the thumb-sucking baby contentedly riding on his arm. "No, I can't give up. I thought so last night, for a while. But having Caron back in my life has shown me miracles are possible, if you want them badly enough. It isn't fair to brush Ramsey off after one clash. If people had done the same to me, I'd a been sunk by now."

"So, what's next, Rick? You want to meet with Ramsey today?" Caron asked hopefully.

"No, not yet."

"But Rick, the world's crashing in on us, on your scheme, on my job...."

"More than you know, honey," he agreed dolefully. "That's why we need some time to recharge. How does a night in the mountains sound? No telephones, no parents, no Granddaddy Bigbucks."

She gaped at him in amazement. "Just take off?"

"Right! We'll take Bobber to the Rockies, to one of those fishing resorts in the foothills," he proposed with new zeal. "We can leave now and easily return later on tomorrow. How does your Monday look?"

"I have a fairly light schedule ahead," she said after a moment of thought. "I planned to concentrate on the baby search."

"Ain't life ironic?" he crowed. "You can focus on the baby face-to-face."

"How will I ever explain my duplicity to the Ramseys?" she wondered in despair. "To my bosses?"

"I'll eventually take those blows for the both of us," Rick insisted. "You and I will never be on opposing sides of anything again, I promise you."

"Oh, you think you can conquer the entire world with those bulging muscles," Eleanor chided, skimming the toast crumbs off the counter with a dishrag.

"I intend to use brainpower this time," Rick informed her with a thrust of his chin.

"The very bulging muscle which gives you the most trouble," Eleanor rejoined.

"I feel funny about running off when this powder keg is about to explode," Caron protested.

"This girl makes sense," Eleanor chimed in.

"It can't explode without the three of us, now can it?" Rick reasoned, stepping closer to Caron. Bobber, true to his name, was bobbing into his chest like an animated doll, unaware of the controversy surrounding him. "We need time together before we face the world. I have things I want to say to you," he said on an intimate note. "I want to clear up your doubts about me. We have to learn to trust each other before outside interference threatens to blow us to smithereens again."

"Again?" she repeated in bleak confusion, smiling as the baby fingered her cloud of hair.

"I'll explain in my own time," he promised quietly.

"You'll be yammering on in explanation for the next century before this thing is through," Eleanor predicted, on tiptoe behind him so as not to be forgotten.

Rick turned in impatience. "May Caron and I yammer on into oblivion together. We've lost enough precious time as it is!"

"I never had anything against you, dear," Eleanor told Caron with effort, determined to budge into their circle.

"There was a time when you and my mother were good friends, Eleanor," Caron reminded her softly.

Eleanor raised her chin high. "But things happened."

"Ma, soon everybody will know everything."

"Heaven help us all!" Eleanor cried in exasperation. "But, if I can be of any help . . ."

"Take my tuxedo back to the cleaners, will ya?" he asked, tugging at the scarf knotted under her chin.

"How'd it fair? Will I be embarrassed out of my mind this time?"

"Not unless you dump something on it yourself," Rick reported with an eye roll.

"Then the insurance was a waste," she huffed. "Money down the drain."

"Speaking of money, please take your sawbuck out of the top pocket of the jacket. Caron didn't charge me a cent for the ride, the party, or the Chinese afterward." Rick beamed in victory when Eleanor, after failing to find a worthy retort, was forced to keep her mouth clamped shut.

"BELIEVE ME, I'M NOT offended by your mother's attempt last night to push money on you. It's kind of sweet the way she clucks over you." Caron chuckled as she dug through her evening bag on her front stoop twenty minutes later. "What I don't like, is that for some reason, the issue of money—the haves and have nots—seems to surround us from all corners."

"How so?" Rick asked, shifting Bobber, cozy in a quilted jacket with a hood tied close to his white moon face, from one arm to another.

"My mother believes wealth is the key to importance as a human being. Your mother believes cash is the weapon to handle us Carlisles. Ramsey obsesses with money and the power it brings."

"That's not everybody."

Caron gripped the doorknob, shoving her key in the lock. "Just wait till Megan gets her hands on you."

"Why?" he asked incredulously.

"The million-dollar reward for leading Ramsey to the baby." Caron pushed open the door, beckoning them into the tiled foyer of the split-entry town house. "Megan believes I deserve part of it for my role in the search. I've tried to explain that I am just the hired help, but—"

"But she isn't having any of it," Megan interrupted, hanging over the wrought-iron railing above them. "If it ain't old Hotshot," she oozed in greeting.

Rick regarded the pert blonde with amusement. "I plan to make sure Caron is rewarded for her efforts."

"Don't forget about the best friend behind the woman," she saucily directed.

"Unlikely, Megan," he conceded, "since you've obviously kept your gutsy wits about you. How've you been?"

"Worried sick about my best friend," she tossed back, her round blue eyes sheeted with relief. "I was afraid she drowned in a vat of rich, syrupy chocolate."

"Megan!" Caron squawked in embarrassment, zipping up five stairs leading to the living area of the house. "He knows."

"You addicted to anything, Meg?" Rick asked, following with the baby.

"I'll never tell," Megan purred. She turned her attention to Caron, now seated on the sofa, in the process of slipping off her high heels. "By the looks of your scuffed shoes, I'd swear you walked to Ramsey's."

Caron reddened. "Quite the opposite as you well know."

"And your dress looks like you crawled there," she pressed the issue with gaiety. "Just wait until your mother sees what's left of her Paul Drake dreams. A stain the size of Utah on your butt. And . . ." She turned her attention back to Rick in unspoken significance.

"Rick Wyatt playing the role of the dashing detective, Drake," he finished neatly with a slight bow at the waist. Bobber thought his movement was a game and squealed for more.

"Isn't he a lamb!" Megan gasped in delight, taking him from Rick's arms. "It's so nice to hold a baby with no health troubles for a change," she cooed. She sat down in an armchair with him, loosening his hood. "So nice to hold a billionaire," she chirped, bouncing him on her knee. "Ooo, your cologne is divine. What do they call it? Oil de bottom?" Bobber sat contented in her lap with a huge grin, obviously enjoying her animation. "So, are you betrothed yet, baby? I'm still free as a bird."

"My brother, Kyle, was asking after you," Rick said, strolling around the sun-drenched room. "He's not rich, but he's trained in many of the niceties that are still beyond Bobber."

"Just because Caron is sold on a Wyatt, doesn't mean I'm as foolish. You guys never knew when to quit—nearly turned the school upside down!"

"I don't appreciate you discussing my love life," Caron put in.

"She's just guessing about the upside-down part," Rick assured. "Go get ready before your mother storms in and upsets my stomach."

"She's called several times already," Megan reported. "Starting at eight o'clock last night."

"What did you say?" Caron demanded.

"Well, the first time I claimed I didn't see your date at all, because you rolled off to fetch him in Ramsey's limo. Boy, did that tickle her! She didn't call back for four hours." At Caron's coaxing gesture, she continued. "The next time I said you were still out. Then this morning I said you were in the shower. Then you were sleeping soundly. The last call was about twenty minutes ago."

"I had better get going," Caron conceded hastily, popping up from the sofa with new energy. "I still have to contact my secretary as well," she murmured half to herself as she moved across the carpet. "Let her know I may not be in till late tomorrow."

"If at all," Rick called out as she disappeared into her bedroom.

"Where are you taking her?" Megan questioned bluntly.

"Maybe it would be easier if you didn't know," he suggested.

"After all the lies I've told in the last twelve hours, I think I can be trusted."

The contradiction of her statement may have escaped her, but Rick couldn't resist chuckling over it.

"We're going to the mountains for the night," Caron called out through the doorway, pulling a lime green sweater over her head before disappearing from view again.

"I'll take good care of her," Rick insisted defensively under Megan's suspicious glare.

Megan scrutinized him over the baby's bright red head. "How can I be sure, Hotshot?"

He balked at her nerve. "Why should I care if you are?"

"Look, Caron is like a sister to me," she explained in quiet reprimand, tossing a look to her bedroom to make certain Caron wasn't in listening range. "I picked up the pieces last time, and though I'd do it again, I'd rather not."

Rick eased down on the arm of her chair, speaking in low tones beneath Bobber's gurgles of glee. "I didn't realize until last night that Caron ever deeply cared for me."

"Well, you can be a lout," she accused.

"What else did I do?" he asked bleakly.

"You told her about our date, for one thing. It really hurt her, Rick, even after all these years."

"Well, she aggravated me to the limit that day," he said in excuse.

"She's liable to do so a lot of the time," Megan cautioned, rocking Bobber from one knee to another as he squirmed for action.

Rick drew a breath of patience. "I was only kidding."

"Well, you sound sincere," Megan relented somewhat dubiously.

"I *am* sincere!"

"It isn't enough on its own," Megan persisted. "This relationship will only work if you understand the Caron psyche."

"I don't follow you," Rick muttered.

Megan shrugged uncomfortably. "What I'm trying to say is that she's normally not impulsive concerning men. She's not into casual flings. Her weakness for you is strictly out of character."

"You make her interest in me sound like a disease," he complained.

"Well, you are accustomed to heating girls into a fever," she teased.

Rick grinned. "You can rest easy over my feelings for Caron."

"They are . . ." she trailed off expectantly.

"They are private and personal for now," he maintained. "If you're looking for thrills of your own, look up Kyle."

"But you're the Wyatt I can't seem to shake from my mind at the moment," she said with sardonic sweetness.

His black brows arrowed suspiciously. "Why?"

"Because of a little wager between two best friends," she snorted rudely. "If it weren't for you I wouldn't be in the jam I'm in with Caron. At the very least, you should consider sending me on an itsy bitsy vacation with some of your reward money." Her lips puckered pitifully. "I will need lots of time to recuperate from the pain and humiliation I am about to suffer at your hands, mister!"

9

"SO, DO YOU THINK you managed to keep the hounds at bay for the next twenty-four hours?" Rick asked Caron a short time later. They were nestled in the cab of his white pickup truck, rolling away from the city. Bobber sat between them, strapped securely to his car seat, gnawing on a teething cookie.

Caron turned her attention from the two-lane road to favor him with a smile. "I left word at my office that I'd be unreachable."

"Unreachable, eh?" Rick winced in pain. "Sounds like an indescribable loss."

Caron's sweet, light laughter filled the cab, causing Bobber to roll his head her way, his round face beaming.

"I think you've got a second fellow falling under your spell," Rick observed fondly.

"I hope so," she said, stroking the baby's velvety cheek. He allowed it from the comfort of Rick's care, favoring her with a small purr. It hurt Caron on a new unexplored level that Bobber was still nervous with her, still often regarded her with guarded eyes. She knew darn well that he didn't even know what he was doing, whom he was rejecting or why. But winning the child's approval had become supremely important to her. It would prove that she could manage babies in general.

Since the beginning of the heir hunt, Caron's mothering instincts had gradually awakened with a niggle here and there. She found herself glancing at babies on the street, wondering if any of them was Douglas Ramsey's grandson. She soon began to notice the differences in them—size, temperament and coloring. Babies became a subject of study. The arrival of Bobber on the scene had taken her from casual interest to hands-on participation. He was her answer to the baby riddle and an important part of Rick's life.

Apparently her time had come to think about raising a family of her own. She understood why her instincts for motherhood had lain dormant until now; with no siblings she had concentrated on the single professional life, gradually distancing herself from married friends with maternal duties. But she couldn't help wondering if it just wasn't in the cards for her. If she failed to befriend this particular baby, how could kid-crazy Rick ever entrust her to bear his children? Would she even have the courage to risk her own baby's rejection? What if, in the end, Rick ended up with Bobber himself and the baby couldn't tolerate her? Would Rick's vow never to let her go again be broken as his prom night one had been?

Her throat was tight with apprehension, but she forced herself to speak. "Rick, is it possible that you could end up with Bobber? Raising him, I mean?"

"It's true that someday I could end up with custody of the Bobber," he theorized with carefully chosen words. "But I highly doubt it's going to happen. Besides, I'm looking forward to fathering children of my own."

Caron gulped under his intent look. "How many?"

Rick released a carefree chuckle. "I'd be bound and determined to keep on going until I land one with a bumpy nose and a fiery quick-draw wit."

Caron returned his easy grin with as much pleasure as she could muster. He was telling her that he wanted her children and expected her to be pleased. If only she had some guarantee that she could be that kind of nurturing caregiver.

They continued on their mountain trek, the Rockies a hazy outline on the horizon as they headed west on 66. The scenery was rustic, farmhouses with smoke curling from their chimneys, combines rolling over the flat farmland, planting winter wheat. They passed through several quaint, small towns, stopping once for a forty-five-cent cup of ice-cold apple cider, and later on for a lunch of trout, delivered fresh to their plates from a mountain stream.

"Estes Park, gateway to the Rocky Mountain National Park," Caron read on a sign as they rolled up to a guard-house leading into the sprawling property. Rick handed the man behind the window five dollars and they continued through the gate.

"Have you been to the Rockies lately?" Rick asked softly over Bobber's dozing form.

"Not in ages," Caron confessed. "But one never forgets the splendor." They continued on the twisting road, wending upward into the majestic mountains. "Do we have a destination?" she asked a short time later. "It's one thing to be impetuous at our age, but we do have the baby along...."

Rick's profile remained glued to the winding road, but the laugh lines around his eyes and mouth crinkled. "Don't worry so much. We have reservations at Pine Cone Cottages, a small resort about twenty minutes from here. It's a getaway of mine, just right for some fishing and relaxation." He paused for a sober moment, as if preparing to say something important to her. "I want you to know I appreciate all of this, Caron."

"What do you mean, Rick?"

"Your willingness to escape on this outing, when you know damn well we're on the hot plate at home. Your blind faith in me and the Bobber. You've been just great since the start. The loyal pal I could always count on years ago. To me, that's every bit as important as the loving."

"Rick, I am anxious to settle that prom issue," she admitted, toying with the handle of her purse.

"We will," he promised.

The sensual quality of his voice made her knees squeeze together in anticipation. Rick always could make everything turn out right. Once Rick decided how he was going to handle Ramsey, they could concentrate on their own personal dreams and ambitions. Whether she had a job at that point was a question that lingered in her mind. A lot. "Rick, you read about the missing heirloom in the paper, didn't you?"

"Yeah, sure."

Rick's angular profile remained steady on the road. "It seemed like a subject best left alone. I imagine it would be impossible for you to continue the search, if you discovered the heirloom in the possession of a certain guy, wouldn't it?" he wagered.

"It would be concrete evidence," she admitted. The last piece to the puzzle—and ruin any chance of returning to the office with a reasonably clear conscience.

The last thing she wanted to see today was that silver dollar!

As it was, the end of the line was coming soon enough. They both knew it.

"You've been doing your job to the best of your ability," he insisted steadfastly.

Not true! If it had been anybody but Rick, she'd have hauled him in to the powers that be on the basis of James's note and the portrait of the nude redhead. They might have laughed her out of the office, but she would've followed through as expected with her trademark methodical investigating and definitive deduction. Rick had a way of twisting her and the issues around his little finger, until she wasn't capable of any rational thought!

Midafternoon they arrived at the resort. It was a small, quaint place sprinkled with ponderosa pines and lush meadowland. Log cabins sat in a crooked line, banking the edge of a meandering stream. Rick continued down the narrow private road to the larger log home sitting at the end of the row. It sported a wide porch across the front. A wooden sign carved with Pine Cone Office hung from the dormer, flapping with every gust of wind.

As Rick popped out of the truck to register, Bobber stirred to life again. The sight of Rick's retreating figure greatly distressed the baby. His moon face quickly reddened and his lower lip quivered in discontent.

"It's all right, Bobber," Caron consoled on a nervous note. "I'm still here."

Bobber, having apparently forgotten about Caron, rolled his head to the right to place the voice. Fear and fury flashed in his china blue eyes as he sized up his situation.

Caron's own lip shook slightly along with her arms as she fumbled with the straps confining him. "Now, little baby," she crooned, "let's be happy together, you and I. After all, I'm all that's standing between you and a cool billion."

He hesitated in uncertainty as she knelt on the seat and awkwardly grasped him under his arms to haul him out of the molded car seat. "Not a whimper now," she pleaded, easing him up and over.

Bobber didn't whimper. He wailed. Squalled at the top of his lungs the second his bottom hit her lap.

Rick emerged from the office minutes later to discover the truck cab empty. His gaze skated the area to find Caron off near a cluster of pines with Bobber in her arms, strolling and singing an off-key tune into the wind. An odd sensation crept through his system at the sight of Caron struggling to win over his little guy, moving him far more profoundly than any of her sexy flirting had. Of course as a novice, she was trying too hard to win the baby over. She was a bundle of nerves and Bobber had been irritated with her all along for that very reason. But she was working on him with passionate resolve.

No wonder she asked if Rick had intentions of raising Bobber. She obviously wanted to be prepared!

Rick realized with sudden certainty that he could never love another human being as much as he loved her at that moment. All her attempts to please—just because he'd asked her to—culminated in a huge knot of emotion, reaching to every fiber of his insides, clear down to the toes of his black boots. He hadn't felt this vulnerable, this frightened, since... Since Caron climbed into the back seat of his Chevy in 1983!

"You pinch that kid or what?" he called out as he crossed the span of gravel. The moment Caron whirled on him, her moist eyes mirroring the Bobber's, he realized he'd been too flippant.

"It isn't funny that babies don't like me," she wailed desperately, depositing Bobber in Rick's arms.

"My mistake," Rick conceded, shifting the baby to his shoulder. "I wanted to help you laugh it off."

"Ha, ha." Caron glared at him, all the more angry as the creases in his cheeks deepened in his effort to suppress his smile. "Just a joke, is it? Watch the spectacle. Watch the fumbling woman pinch the baby? Watch the—"

"Watch the most delightful, most endearing sight I've ever seen," Rick quietly interrupted.

"What?" she cried in confusion, wiping her cheeks with the back of her hand.

"With all you've conquered in your life, you're crushed that this baby doesn't warm to you."

"How can I have babies of my own if they're going to cry the moment I touch them?" she wondered bleakly.

"Aw, c'mere, Quick Draw," he murmured in invitation, drawing her close to make it a threesome. Bobber's sniffles filled her ear as he rested his forehead against her hair. "You went to school for a zillion years to become an attorney, exerting an enormous amount of patience and energy, I'm sure. You have to give this child care thing a chance with at least a fraction of that zest."

Caron rested her head on his chest in exhaustion. "What if I can't do this?"

"You can," he asserted. "Your desire is the main thing. Bobber can sense you're nervous, that's all. And I think he misses his mother," he added in honesty. "As it happens, she will be coming around tomorrow to rescue him."

"Oh, Rick." Caron released a breath of relief, burrowing her cheek into the denim of his jacket.

"In the meantime we're going to enjoy our day. By the time we head back, I can guarantee Bobber will be your best buddy." When she lifted a dubious brow, he set the baby back in her arms. Bobber's head spun at Rick in betrayal. "This is your call, man," he said, ruffling his red hair. "The hottest babe in the woods wants you. Don't blow it."

Bobber accepted his fate, just as long as he could keep an eye on Rick. Caron made certain he could, trailing Rick back to the truck as he retrieved their suitcases.

Their log cabin proved to be a warm, two-room affair with braided rugs, a wood-burning stove, a kitchenette, a double bed and a miniscule bathroom.

While the baby slept off his exhaustion in his portable crib in the kitchen, Rick settled down on the creaky steel-framed bed in the bedroom.

"Shouldn't we be doing something else?" Caron asked halfheartedly as Rick pulled her against his length.

"Like what?" he rumbled in discontent.

"I don't know," Caron murmured, nipping his shoulder through his T-shirt. "Unpack or something. It *is* the afternoon."

"Take a page from Bobber's book," Rick suggested, twirling a lock of her silky hair around his finger. "When he's tired, he conks out."

"And when he's angry, he bellers," Caron added meditatively, running a finger along Rick's mustache. "Maybe there is something to be said for expressing one's feelings more openly, as a baby does naturally."

"I love you, baby," Rick groaned contentedly, squeezing her close. "And I can't stop the urge to show you how much. Especially on this nice, cozy bed . . ."

"All I've ever wanted was to be a part of everything you are," she said softly, nipping at his ear.

Rick couldn't help but notice, however, that there was something quite wicked dancing in her gem green eyes. "What's going on in that pretty little noggin?" he asked.

"I was just thinking, Rick. For the first time in this girl's memory, you look like a desperate teen!"

"You put that look there, lady," he growled wolfishly. "You'll have to wipe it away. Over and over again, I hope."

"Sounds like a long-term job," she huffed in exasperation.

"Sounds like a marriage proposal," he corrected, moving his thumb across her chin.

She gaped in amazement. "You're asking, right now?"

"I can't think of a better time, considering I've already asked you to have my baby."

"Oh, you mean the bumpy-nosed one with the quick wit?" she sought to clarify with feigned innocence.

"I do. And any others that may turn up."

"How can I refuse such a romantic offer?" Caron dropped her lips back to his, melding her limbs into his length.

"Oh, Caron," he rasped, tearing his lips from her mouth. "I've missed you in my life."

"Why didn't you call me before now?" she asked, desperate to understand.

He frowned thoughtfully. "Because I didn't want to be turned down, I guess. Didn't want to find out you weren't that angel I remembered. Then the heir situation came along and Kyle told me you worked at snap, crackle, pop. The coincidence seemed too incredible not to be fateful. It seemed like a second chance for us."

"You didn't sound too interested on the telephone," she recalled dryly.

"I always come on too smart. Especially when I'm scared. Believe me, calling you was one of the most courageous things I've ever done. I was hoping for instant harmony. All I got was your instant suspicion. True to nature I blew a fuse. Couldn't handle the bickering with my heart split in two over James and everything."

"And then I showed up at your place."

"Something I never expected you to do!"

"I couldn't leave it alone," she admitted.

"Not you!" he agreed in dour adamancy, tweaking her nose. "I just expected the cops, or the bar association, or the Mounties, or Ramsey himself. But you charged at me in person. Set me up for the fall in your snug, racy suit and little yellow hat." He rolled his eyes with an unsteady sigh. "You've always been a singeing heat in some very uncomfortable places inside of me."

"Good."

Rick's heart began to pound harder as Caron sat up to straddle him, digging her jean-clad thighs into his rib cage. She took the initiative by pulling off his T-shirt and gently clawing through his dense chest hair with her tiny fingernails. He pulsed with anticipation as she slowly, slowly raked upward to his nipples, beading them with rapid little scrapes. With a lazy-eyed look she drew her mouth to the small dark circles to lavish them with long wet sucks, her hands again roaming free on his pink, sensitized skin.

Just when he thought the hair on his chest was going to ignite into a forest blaze, she ever so slowly uncurled on his length. Soon she was pressing her pelvis into his arousal, stimulating his lower body to an equally aching madness through their layers of confining clothing. With frenzied frustration he ran his large hands down her spine, pushing up her lime green sweater, kneading the gentle curve of her bottom deeper and deeper into him.

Caron's breath came in hard, fast puffs as his arousal grew beneath her.

"I'm not a man who likes restraints," he complained heavily, unclasping her bra, reaching up to peel it and her sweater off with one fluid motion.

"Mmm . . ." With a heady moan of need, Caron arched her back so he could unbuckle and unsnap the lower barriers between them. Since the urgency was his this time, Rick first slid his pants off, kicking them aside with amazing dexterity. He then reached back down to unfasten her zipper, tugging the layers of fabric down over her hips to reveal creamy, satin skin.

Heat as intense as the sun beating down on the roof burned them as they ever so slowly ignited in afternoon lovemaking. Unlike the last time on the dryers in the dead of night, or the first time in the back seat of Rick's car, they were on brilliant display for daytime exploration.

Caron was like a pliable kitten as she rolled off him, tucking herself underneath his body for a long, liquid kiss. Rick slowly tasted the recesses of her mouth, his hands cupping her face. When he started to shift position on the bed, he felt her hands pressing him back down on her. He would've thought it was his skin-grazing appeal, if not for the flash of uncertainty in her eyes.

"What's the matter, honey?" he asked gently, teasing her lower lip with his thumb.

Caron rolled her head on the pillow, blinking to avoid his eyes. "Nothing. Just love me, Rick. Like this. Right now."

"You're still self-conscious about your body," he second-guessed in awe.

"Only without clothes!" she confessed in a squeak.

"But we made unbridled love last night," he chided.

"But it was dark. . . ." she stumbled in explanation.

Rick gaped in disbelief. "My sweet, innocent darling. If you had any idea just how attractive you really are . . . you'd really be dangerous!" Deaf to her murmurs of protest, Rick rolled off her. With one arm propped under him, he took leisurely perusal of her lanky nude form, stretched out in ivory splendor before him on the worn blue sheet.

"Rick—"

"Hush, now," he crooned, evading her swatting hand to stroke the curve of her thigh. His touch traveled up to the juncture of her womanhood, caressing the wispy V in the breadth of his huge palm. Satisfied with her sigh of pleasure, he continued his leisurely trip to her navel, then on to her slightly rounded breasts.

"Thank goodness she didn't tamper with you two beauties," he said, kissing the small fleshy mounds with a grateful smack. When she released a relaxed laugh, he kissed them again and again, tantalizing her nerve endings to the breaking point. "You can trust me all the way, my love," he assured hoarsely. "My beautiful, beautiful love."

In the midst of his sweet torment, she moved her hand to his arousal, skimming his solid shaft with light-hard pressure. When he stopped for a breath, she exploited his vulnerability, tipping him over on the mattress.

"Wench!" he growled, reeling back on the bank of pillows. She followed his fall, landing on his chest with a thud, locking her lips on his before he could regroup. After a dizzying kiss, she sat up again on his abdomen, guiding him deeply inside her. He smiled. Her new belief in her beauty was the cause of his incredible happiness. Or at least the second reason.

"This what you had in mind?" she asked, tipping her head back with new abandon.

"Give it to me," he ordered thickly.

With hands gripping his massive shoulders, Caron moved over him. Fevered impulsion soon brought them to a heart-hammering climax. They collapsed together in the soft, cushy mattress.

"Now this is what I call an afternoon nap," Rick groaned in pleasure, gently stroking her back.

Bobber's cry suddenly bounced off the walls of the cabin.

"Nap time's over," Caron declared on a sigh, slowly raising herself from the bed, scanning the floor for her clothing.

"I dearly love that kid, but in some ways I will be extremely glad when his mom comes back for him," Rick grumbled, swinging his legs over the side of the bed. "Coming, you little siren!" he called out.

"Our own children will no doubt be a bit of an inconvenience on occasion," she predicted, tossing him his rumpled briefs and jeans.

"Yeah," he conceded, impatiently tangling with the clothing as Bobber squalled all the louder. "But at least I'll have the pleasurable memory of making them myself!"

AFTER TREATING BOBBER to a snack of applesauce and a diaper change, the trio took a walk along the stream running behind the cabins. Bobber rode in an infant carrier on Rick's back, his round blue eyes glowing as brightly as the azure skies above them. Caron had had the foresight to bring along her camera. With Bobber's hand-clapping approval, she began to take candid shots of the boys and the scenery.

"When we get back to the cabins, we'll have to ask the owner to take a few group shots of the three of us," Rick proposed. "It'll give us something to remember this crazy little triangle of ours."

Caron could read the regret in his eyes. Whatever was in store tomorrow concerning Bobber, Rick was seeing it as a loss. It was understandable. He was just wild about the child. To have a child with him . . .

"So, tell me more about this bet between you and Megan," Rick prompted in a change of subject, taking careful steps on the dirt trail.

"I was wondering when you were going to bring it up," she said in a knowing tone, matching his effort to be light-hearted.

"She sure was in a huff about it."

"Well, you don't have to look so smug over her misfortune," Caron chided, the dimples deepening in her cheeks.

Rick shrugged his broad shoulders. "Guess I just can't help myself."

"Then you don't deserve to know the details," she proclaimed, turning on the heels of her hiking shoes, trotting farther up the dirt trail winding into the hills.

Rick caught up in a few easy strides, trapping Caron from behind in a bear hug. "You'll talk, missy," he muttered in mock menace against her fragrant fluff of hair. "We have our ways, don't we, Bobber?"

Caron twisted out of his arms, turning to face a pair of laughing faces. "If this innocent only knew of the things you involve him in," she cooed.

"He's just one of the guys," he retorted, reaching back to tug at the visor on the baby's bonnet-style cap.

"All right," Caron surrendered. "Megan and I made a pact back in school. Foolishly, of course," she added.

"Let us be the judge," he directed, arms folded across his chest.

Caron stared off into the horizon at the looming mountains with a reminiscent grin. "Well, we made a wager over which one of us would get a phone call from you first."

"You did?" he asked in boyish delight.

"Of course we thought the chances of it occurring faded years ago," she assured him in a downplaying tone. "I just happened to have kept the signed agreement stuffed away inside my yearbook."

"Held out for me all this time," he boasted.

"It was forgotten there, Rick," she insisted.

"Sure, sure," he agreed with a wave of dismissal.

"Pressed into the pages with my old activity pass!"

"Hope you're listening to this, Bobber," he advised under his breath. "This is the same kind of stuff that is going to happen to you, man."

Caron sighed in exasperation at the sight of Bobber focused on a scampering chipmunk. "He couldn't care less, Rick."

"Babies are a wonder of miracles," Rick retorted. "He may remember my advice when he really needs it."

"Heaven help him!" Caron lamented, throwing her hands in the air.

"Hey, for the class rebel, I haven't done so bad, have I?" he challenged, cuffing her chin. "I've got a great business. Lots of family and friends. And now the circle is complete with the girl of my dreams. The Bobber could do worse."

He guided her mouth to his for a leisurely kiss. Caron closed her eyes, savoring the sweetness of his lips, all the while aware of the added attraction of a fat little finger exploring the curve of her ear.

"So what does the loser of the bet have to do?" Rick asked, releasing her lips with a smack.

Caron gazed at him with twinkling green eyes. "It would spoil the fun to tell in advance."

"Not fair!"

"You're the one double-dealing," she argued. "You've been running up an enormous credit line on trust. I want to hear about the prom, Hotshot, right now! Why didn't you come for me?" Caron knew the pain she was feeling was expressed vividly on her torn-up face. But he wouldn't dodge the issue any longer. "It won't affect our future, if that's what you're afraid of," she added to soften her flare-up. "As I told you, I understand about teenage boys now—"

"Well, you don't understand about me, Caron," he cut in. "And in this case, I think the pain was spread out pretty equally." Despite her noises of confusion, he kept his silence as he grasped her elbow, guiding her to the grassy ground banking the stream. "Let's sit here for a little while. Watch the water roll."

Caron obligingly sat beside him on the hard ground, reaching over to dab Bobber's runny nose with a tissue. "It's not like you to be at a loss for words," she prodded in complaint.

"I know the words. Expressing them is the problem." Rick kept his eyes on the rushing waters sparkling in the sunshine for a long, pensive moment. He eventually turned to her, his dark eyes steady and warm. "You see, Caron, it just so happens that you won that bet of yours ten years ago."

"What!"

"To tell you the truth, it's still painful for me to remember. And I've never told another living soul," he confided with difficulty. "Except Ma."

Caron placed her hand on his raised knee, peering at him expectantly. "You called me?"

"Just like I promised. Got the brush-off from your mother. She said you were sleeping or something."

"So you gave up?"

"So I came over," he quickly corrected. "Tangled with Deborah in person."

"Why didn't you tell me this sooner?" she gasped in dismay.

"And let her wreck all the good stuff?" he demanded in endearing indignation. "Not on your life! Nope, I figured there was no rush."

"And what if I had hesitated as you hauled me up on the dryers?" she asked wryly.

"I don't know! Guess I just hoped—and rightly so—that you'd be too turned on to ask questions. I knew this moment would come soon enough, if everything worked out."

Caron thought about the revelation, anger surging through her system. "My mother's interference knows no bounds! I'd like to get my hands on her this very minute."

"Which is one reason why I've chosen to tell you miles away from the city," he explained. "We have to settle this between ourselves. Drawing her into it is only secondary in importance."

"If you did care, Rick, why didn't you come back the next day or the next?" she persisted, her heart constricting in pain.

Rick sighed deeply, covering the hand on his knee before she could snatch it away. "Caron, your mother was as rude and mean as she could be about it—"

"The rebel succumbs to Deborah's tirade," she interrupted in disappointment.

"Worse," he confessed. "Deb shot some points home that I simply couldn't argue."

"Like what, Rick?"

"Emotionally, I was set to fight for you, Caron," he declared fiercely. "You did crazy things to my heart and I cherished you as I did no one else. But your mother wounded me with the truth. I had an attitude problem. I took what I wanted. You, on the other hand, were extremely mature, directed. Then she pinned me down about the future." Rick shot Caron a helpless look. "My intentions didn't extend past the weekend. I'd always gotten by on the seat of my pants."

"Your rejection shattered me completely!" she cried woundedly.

"I didn't know!" Rick maintained defensively. "It never occurred to me back then. You just seemed to have your act so together. She was very persuasive on that count. Said I'd only be an anchor in your life, that you were a brilliant girl with a full scholarship to Harvard. Harvard! You never told anybody about that, Caron."

"I was already known as the bookworm of the student council," Caron said in defense, "while you were regarded as the shining rebel knight fighting for student rights. I couldn't have stood the extra heckling."

"Well, Deb did a full number on me about messing with your future," Rick went on. "Said you were destined for great things. Hell, she was pushing all my buttons. She knew if you'd given me your virginity, you'd give me a whole lot more. I was slapped down properly. Figured she was right. I didn't have what it takes to handle a bundle of brains like you."

"How awful for you," Caron conceded in sympathy.

Rick shook his head dazedly. "Then she moved in for the kill. Insisted that my glory days were over the minute I grabbed my diploma. That the popular rebels like me who floated through high school with charm and arrogance never grew up, that we were the burger flippers and floor scrubbers. She said wallflower scholars like you made the world go round and would eventually shine as responsible adults. By the time I walked away from your house, I wasn't sure I had the skills to direct my feet home."

"She never said a word," Caron whispered numbly. "She knew how I cried. Pretended it didn't matter." Caron put her fists to her eyes to blot out the memory.

"She thought it was the right thing to do," Rick offered in fairness. "But I've never understood why she didn't appreciate your beauty as well as your brains. What a tragedy."

"She has dwelled on my unattractiveness since child-hood," Caron admitted. "I've never been able to shake that feeling of physical inadequacy."

"You've always been the most desirable creature on earth to me," he murmured huskily.

"Oh, how her lecture must have hurt."

"It was a hell of a graduation present," he confirmed soberly, "learning you're a has-been at eighteen. Though it wasn't her intention, it turned out to be just the jump start I needed. I wasn't about to give up the respect of my peers—my own self-respect."

"So you went out and earned the admiration of the en-tire neighborhood," Caron finished with a smug nod.

Rick grinned. "Eventually. I enrolled in vocational school, pooled my mechanical abilities with some train-ing. I worked at a car dealership for a couple years, saving my money for a business of my own. The building hous-ing the shoe store came up for sale and the rest is history."

"The neighborhood really needed a Laundromat," Caron agreed. "And a place to socialize. Hotshots is a very inventive combination."

"Don't pass the word about our rendezvous atop the dryers," he cautioned in teasing sternness. "If the sideline were to catch on, I'd have the vice squad after me!"

Caron's eyes slitted naughtily. "Don't worry, darling. The only person I'd like to lure to the dryers is my mother. A nice hot tumble inside number seven might be just the thing to shake her to her senses!"

Rick sighed wistfully. "I've often wondered what would have happened if you had opened the door on that day so long ago."

"What if?" She squeezed his hand. "All we can do now is move on together, grateful for the second chance."

"Yep. And speaking of second chances, I want you to help me unharness this critter from his upper deck seat," Rick said, reaching around to playfully poke Bobber in the tummy. "He's in extremely good spirits right now, making it your perfect time for some intensive Bobber bonding."

When Caron reached for the baby this time, it was with a far steadier grip. To their relief, Bobber took the transfer like a trooper, pressing his hands into Caron's cheeks. She promptly rewarded him with a kiss.

"Whoa, there, partner," Rick cautioned in a teasing voice. "You got a lip-lock on my babe." When they nuzzled and giggled on, paying no attention to his complaint, Rick did the only thing he could think of. He snapped some pictures of them. About a dozen or so.

10

"I DON'T LIKE THIS, Rick." Caron's tone was ominous as she and Bobber stood beside him on the sidewalk in front of Hotshots late Monday afternoon. They'd just returned from their trip to the Rockies and a Closed sign hung in the front window, wedged between the glass and the tilted wooden blinds. Rick had no intention of changing his mind about his master plan, either. No amount of cajoling from Caron would sway him.

"Stay here, troops," he directed, popping inside for a brief look around. Satisfied that everything was undisturbed, he joined them back on the sidewalk, moving toward the street door leading directly to his second-floor apartment. Caron was right on his heels, Bobber resting in the hollow of her hip, a huge diaper bag swinging from her shoulder.

"Figure it this way," she proposed anxiously, "if they were meant to be a lifelong item, fate would've brought them back together, too."

Rick set the portable crib against the brick building and turned to plant a kiss on her perfectly pert nose. "Fate is sort of forcing them together, Quick Draw. Wily old Cupid plans to make them in-laws."

They took on the steep staircase with all of Bobber's belongings, debating the parent issue all the way. Bobber, now content in a newfound friendship with Caron, leaned comfortably into her torso, a thumb planted firmly in his mouth. His trust had become immensely important to her, making it all the more important that he have just the right future—with or without Douglas Ramsey.

"Set him in his high chair," Rick requested, moving through the small apartment, switching on lights. "We'll heat up his grub and get those prizefighters over here for the final face-off."

"What if one won't come?" Caron asked doubtfully, securing a bib around the baby's neck. "After we've invited the other," she added for effect.

Rick paused in the center of his kitchen, clutching a baby bottle and a jar of strained carrots. "Just which one do you think would turn down the opportunity to sound off to this audience?" he wondered incredulously.

"Which indeed?" Caron laughed in surrender. "You don't even know what's funny, Bobber," she added in a teasing note as he mimicked her.

"You call Deb the debutante first," he suggested, moving to the microwave. "She can probably run faster than my ma, but she has more miles to cover."

Eleanor Wyatt was the first to arrive about a half hour later, her round, cheery face set in uncharacteristic discontent. "Deb wouldn't dare show up here," she proclaimed as she crossed the threshold. "No offense to you, Caron," she added with a small nod in the younger woman's direction. She peeled off her woolen coat, swiftly settling into Rick's wooden rocker with Bobber and a book of fairy tales.

"Now Ma—" Rick began, only to be interrupted by the front buzzer. Caron moved to the door to find her mother on the other side.

"Caron!" Deborah exclaimed. Despite her warrior stance, her shell of stiff gold hair was slightly mussed and her kelly green suit a trifle rumpled. "I don't understand any of this," she hissed in her daughter's ear. "I've been in constant touch with Megan since Saturday night, begging for news of you. Then you call with this preposterous summons. What on earth could Richard Wyatt have to do with you? Is he up on charges or something? Does he need an attorney?"

"Rick isn't in any trouble," Caron said under her breath, casting a quick glance back into the apartment to see if the Wyatts could hear their exchange. By the set of Rick's shoulders in the kitchen doorway, she was sure he could. "We spent last night together in the Rockies."

"But what of the charming Paul Drake?" she desperately demanded.

"There is no Paul Drake, Mother. Rick is the one who called you for my number."

"That's fraud!"

"That's entertainment," Rick corrected with a cutting, mirthful edge.

"You didn't take *him* to the Ramsey affair, did you?" Deborah demanded in despair with the thrust of a manicured finger. "No wonder Megan's been giving me the brush-off! How can you be falling for him again, Caron? Your professional reputation will be tarnished!"

"It most certainly will not," Caron scoffed hotly. "Rick is a reputable businessman. And even if he weren't, I'd still want him just because."

"Come away with me now," Deborah urged.

Caron held firm as Deborah attempted to pull her out on the landing. "You won't pull us apart again, Mother. I love him. Still love him," she corrected.

Deborah released her with a bleak cry. "Why him? Why now, after all these years?"

"Come in and find out," Caron invited with a sweeping hand.

"Seems I have no choice!" Deborah shot past her daughter into the living room, a well-dressed locomotive of fury.

"Hello, Deborah," Eleanor greeted flatly.

Deborah slowly drank in the sight of Eleanor, seated in the rocking chair with the baby in her lap, and the array of baby things scattered around the apartment. She whirled back on Caron on the verge of explosion.

Rick sauntered closer, his arms folded across his expansive chest. Clad in a white T-shirt and faded blue jeans, with his dark eyes burning and his mouth curled sardonically, he was an older version of the rebel she knew and resented.

Deborah eyed him warily. "Indulged in some free-lance fatherhood I see, Richard."

"Ricky did no such thing," Eleanor countered in indignation. "He—"

"Ma, please," Rick cut in, extending a stifling hand. "The Bobber's legit, Deborah," he informed her easily. "Legit by even your standards."

"I imagine you told Caron everything," Deborah deduced on a plainly unapologetic note as her gaze shifted from Caron's granite expression to Rick's smug one.

"I am so disappointed in you, Mother," Caron said tersely.

"I did what I thought best," Deborah staunchly maintained.

Caron shook her head in pity. "You've always tried to control me."

"You were a child back then, Caron," Deborah fired back. "I did what I thought should be done to ensure your future. You've always had a quick wit, a brilliant mind. You needed to nourish your intellect, not your libido."

Her mother's blunt remark scalded her to the core, but she sought to control her temper. This was a fight she could win hands down, by just being in the right. "You should've trusted my brilliance then, Mother. Trusted me to decide my own fate."

"A young girl infatuated with the class hunk?" she spat in disbelief.

Rick drew a huge cynical smile. "Thank you for the compliment. As you know, good looks are essential in the race for social supremacy."

"Shut up, son," Eleanor intervened.

He murmured a suspect apology, stepping closer to Caron in support. The last thing he wanted was a face-off between the Wyatts and the Carlisles. Caron was on his team. Permanently.

Deborah attempted to put her arms around her daughter's stiff body. "I love you with all my heart and wanted you to have every opportunity to succeed," she babbled in justification. "I couldn't let you throw it all away for some passionate affair."

"You don't know that I would have," Caron urged, using her elbow as a buffer between them.

Deborah's face crumpled as if fancying herself the injured party. "But I couldn't take the chance, don't you see? Yes, perhaps Rick Wyatt was momentarily interested. But what if he became bored with what you had to offer? Boys that age only appreciate a fancy wrapping. They—"

"She did have a fancy wrapping!" Rick cut in again sharply. "You're the one who's held her back, Deborah, always insinuating that she had only brains to see her through life. That she was plain and could only aspire to beauty."

"Stay out of it, Ricky!" Eleanor scolded. "We all can see Caron's never been prettier."

Rick's patience evaporated. "Forget it, Ma! Caron needs my assurances until she learns that she's a lovely woman inside and out. Until Deborah stops pressing her own image of beauty on Caron."

"Why, I never!" Deborah blurted out in instant denial.

"For heaven sakes, Deb," Eleanor huffed, ignoring her own advice against interference, "has any one of us ever met your standards?"

"I only strive for the best," Deborah maintained, studying her flawless nails.

"Always strived for something better, you mean," Eleanor corrected. "You've been blind to the best. It's been under your very nose all these years. A wonderful husband, a devoted daughter. And a group of true friends— whom you chose to abandon," she added with a wounded look.

"Well," Deborah said with a sniff, "I've always felt that our break would have been a clean one had the children not fought the night of the prom."

"Hey, don't you dare blame us for your problems," Caron swiftly interceded.

"Your girl is right," Eleanor admitted. "We used them as an excuse. So, have you found better friends in your new neighborhood?"

"Not better," Deborah confessed. "But I do like change, Elly. You and the girls have always been content with staying close to home, hanging around this neighborhood. 'Tisn't enough for me."

"Mother, I fear you will never have enough of anything," Caron told her sadly. "I know I certainly will never please you."

Deborah reared back in shock. "Why, Caron, is this the way you really feel?"

Caron nodded with difficulty. "You always push things too far, Mom. You believe in me only to a point, even now."

"But I'm so proud of you, dear."

"You are *almost* pleased, *almost* proud. Perfection, to you, is always just around the corner."

"You have an attitude problem, Deborah," Rick informed her. "Take it from the attitude expert."

Deborah's face contorted in fury. "How dare you invade my life this way?"

"I dare because I intend to take you on as my mother-in-law," he announced, baring a row of white teeth under his slash of a black mustache.

Deborah clutched her heart as though shot point-blank. "You don't mean it!"

"We're taking the vows, all right," Rick affirmed, glowing under her mortified look. "To love, honor and banter with the best of 'em for the rest of our days."

"But you've been out of touch for ten years," Deborah sputtered. "How can you possibly be sure it's right?"

"Because we took that long journey separately, Mother," Caron promptly informed her with pride. "We've known others and no one quite compares."

"Ditto for me, Mother Deborah," Rick agreed.

She shot him a lethal look. "Don't ever call me that! What about your career, Caron?" she attempted to reason. "Your social connections to people like the Ramseys?"

"I don't plan to fall into a dark hole after the wedding," Caron retorted, embarrassed by her mother. "I love my work and I will continue practicing law."

"Are you still so concerned with the cream of the crop?" Eleanor challenged. She rose from the rocker with Bobber, gently depositing him in his playpen. "Of course you must be, sending a limousine into the neighborhood to pick up my son."

Deborah blinked in confusion.

"Don't play innocent with me," Eleanor scolded, hands on her ample hips. "Caron picked Ricky up Saturday night in a stretch limo. It reeks of your highfalutin ways!"

"If I had a limousine, I'd have ridden past your place myself," Deborah snapped back.

"Probably honking the horn to the tune of 'Yankee Doodle Dandy,'" Eleanor snorted.

"A job for my chauffeur," Deborah corrected.

"You two are having the time of your lives ripping into each other," Caron observed in horror.

"Who can make a better job of it than two ex-friends?" Deborah reasoned with a satisfied nod.

"Or two future in-laws?" Eleanor chimed in, to Deborah's chagrin. "I managed to live with all of your airs before you moved away," she acknowledged graciously. "I imagine I can adjust once again."

"Well, my style was okay when you wanted help choosing a wallpaper pattern or a new dress," Deborah reminded her.

"Yes, you do have a certain flair," Eleanor relented. "But it doesn't mean you know everything."

"I know you could look ten years younger if you tinted your gray hair brown and wore heels rather than those rubber soles," Deborah observed with sharp inspection.

"Lots of the movie stars have gone completely gray," Eleanor maintained with a sniff. "And I have weak arches. You know about my arches, Deborah."

"And scarves are out as headwear," Deborah added, spying the plaid one tossed over Eleanor's coat on the sofa. "O-U-T!"

"Why—You are O-U-T!" Eleanor frothed, pointing to the door. "As of right now."

"Very well." Deborah stepped rapidly to the door. "But this isn't over yet."

"I won't be turned away this time, Deb," Rick warned, winding a thick protective arm around Caron. "I've got nothing but pride in myself now. I'm quite worthy of being the son-in-law of the illustrious Deborah Carlisle."

Caron turned to him as the door slammed shut after her. "What have we done to her, Hotshot?" she wailed in worry.

"Given her a dose of real life," Eleanor piped up. "Don't you fret, Deb will come around." She leaned over to stroke Bobber's head with a loving hand. "Perhaps not in time for the wedding, but certainly in time for the first birth. Not even that dragon could resist a precious one like you," she cooed at the child.

"Ma!" Rick protested. "Let me get a ring on her finger first." But he was pleased over the prospect of his mother fussing over his baby sometime in the future. Caron could see it in those delicious dark eyes of his.

CARON ARRIVED at the office Tuesday morning to find it a hubbub of activity. She paused at her secretary's desk just as the pleasant, middle-aged woman was setting the telephone back in its cradle.

"Good morning, Glenny," Caron said cheerily, edging her hip against Glenda Bain's desk to examine the telephone messages thrust into her hands. "I see half of these are from Mr. Ramsey," she noted, thumbing through the yellow squares of paper.

"The other half are from his sister, Agatha," Glenda reported, picking up the telephone as it buzzed again. "Sharp, Krandell and Peterson," she rattled off. "Oh, yes,

Mr. Ramsey," she said, her eyes rising to her immediate superior for on-the-spot direction.

Caron raised a finger to her lips, then reached for the open appointment book on Glenda's desk to scan her schedule.

"Yes, sir, I can assure you that she's expected in today," the secretary efficiently hedged. "She hasn't reached her desk yet, however...."

Caron set the book back down on the cluttered desktop, pointing to the open space at one o'clock. Glenda swiftly relayed the message and hung up.

"He didn't like the delay," Glenda said with a cringe. "He was already chomping at the bit yesterday, along with the sister."

"He's current with all of the claims of last week," Caron complained. "But," she relented, "the man is accustomed to snapping his fingers for immediate action. So, how did the interviewing go without me yesterday?" she asked brightly, forcing herself to keep up the pretense of the search. She hoped by day's end Bobber's mother would be back and things would be settled.

Glenda nodded with a smile. "I put that sharp paralegal in charge of the interviews just as you instructed. He filled out the questionnaires according to your specifications. I must say, there are a few possibilities," Glenda informed her hopefully, rolling back in her chair to retrieve them from the bottom drawer of the file cabinet behind her. "You'll find a couple possibilities in there," she said quietly, setting the folders in Caron's outstretched arms. "Medals, I mean. It sure would help if we knew exactly what sort we were looking for."

"Mr. Ramsey's simply trying to protect himself from any flimflam," Caron offered in excuse. She hadn't told a soul at the firm that she knew the medal to be a silver dollar, fearing Douglas would be angry with Agatha for spilling the beans. At the rate the secrets were mounting, Caron feared she would soon burst. "Can't trust anybody these days with a billion at stake," she said with a laugh. "Not even one's lawyer."

"He's got the best in you, Caron," Glenda proclaimed.

Caron shot her a crooked grin. "I guess we can allow him some slack under the circumstances just the same. We all have a confidence or two we believe is best kept."

"Let me know if you wanna trade a few," Glenda teased, twirling a pencil in her hand.

Caron stopped short by the door to her office with a sudden afterthought. "By the way, keep on the lookout for my personal photos. I left them at the one-hour place downstairs and they'll be sending them up."

"Will do," Glenda promised, reaching again for the ever-ringing telephone.

Caron spent the morning going through the motions of examining the claims. Like last week's batch, yesterday's ranged from outrageous to pathetic to downright hilarious. Douglas Ramsey would be demanding answers from Rick and her in short order. The idea of snowing a man like Ramsey had been insane since its inception. How could Rick have been so arrogant? So infuriating? So damn stubborn?

He was born to it, that's how! Rick Wyatt had been a rebel with one cause or another since they were kids. Of course this time the cause hadn't been a self-serving exercise in wit, but fought in the name of another. Rick had done it for James Ramsey. He'd acted altruistically out of loyalty, out of friendship.

Caron propped her chin in her hands, closing her eyes with a soulful sigh. Is that how she would explain it, when the whole scam blew? Would Ramsey have empathy for

Rick's allegiance to James? For her allegiance to Rick? Maybe her career at the firm would be over. Maybe she'd have to brush up on her two-step and look at dryers three through seven as a business commodity rather than a hotbed of lust.

When Caron returned from her quick lunch at the café downstairs, the Ramseys were already comfortably ensconced in her office. Ramsey was pacing about; Agatha sat on the small sofa opposite her desk.

"No one outside so we just came in," Ramsey explained.

"Hope you don't mind, Caron," Agatha chirped, eyes twinkling behind wired reading glasses. Her small feet were up on the cushions, case files heaped around her. "We just couldn't wait to see this latest slew of contestants."

"Contestants, sister?" Ramsey's bushy gray brows lifted over the rims of his glasses. "This is not 'The Dating Game.'"

"No, it's like 'The Match Game,'" Agatha tittered, sparing Caron a wink as she goaded him on. "Match up the itsy bitsy baby with the right medal, then match up the old grouchy billionaire with the baby."

"A fool at ninety," Ramsey muttered.

"A crusty buzzard at seventy-seven," she tossed back gaily.

"Any prospects in this batch?" Caron asked dutifully.

"Not yet," Ramsey replied in a bark, wandering over to the windows with his meaty hands clasped behind his back.

Caron set her purse on the desktop, doing a double take as Agatha's thin, veined hands shifted through the files atop the cushion. Lodged in the stack was a large colorful envelope. An envelope from Rapid One Hour Photo on the main floor of the building.

"Why, what on earth is this?" Agatha squeaked in girl-ish curiosity. With surprisingly nimble fingers, she pulled open the sticky flap of the envelope.

Her pictures! Bobber's photograph was inside that en-velope! Caron's heart hammered in her chest as she thought back to the nude portrait of Agatha, to her milky white skin, her reams of brilliant red hair. The resem-blance might mean nothing to the elderly woman, or it might just be the key.

"Those are personal pictures of mine," Caron said cheerily, rounding the desk as fast as her beige heels and tight brown skirt would allow. "A friend and I took a trip to the Rockies over the weekend and—"

"So that's where you were yesterday," Ramsey charged with the noises of an irate parent.

"Why, yes. But believe me, the search moved on effi-ciently." Caron reached for the envelope in Agatha's hand, but failed to take firm hold of the flap. The pictures spilled forth, spreading over the carpeting. Agatha swiftly swung her small legs over the side of the sofa to help with the re-trieval.

"Oh, my stars!" Agatha's half glasses slipped to the tip of her nose as she took one of the pictures featuring the threesome.

"The owner of the resort took it," Caron ventured awkwardly—and uselessly, she soon realized. Agatha was caught up in her own thoughts. Specifically distressing thoughts, for the old woman's complexion was growing pasty under the rouge splashes on her cheeks, and her eyes were welling with tears.

"Look, Douglas," she gasped hoarsely, motioning to her brother with a jerky, bejeweled hand.

Douglas Ramsey strode swiftly to her side. "Why, I see nothing, woman," he rumbled impatiently, after raising the photograph to his face for a good look. "Except that Rick Wyatt was with you, Caron. No wonder I couldn't track him down! What's this? There's a baby riding on his shoulder in some sort of sack." The old man's look was sharp and suspicious. "Where the blazes did he come from? He's mine, isn't he?"

"His name is Bobber and he isn't yours, Mr. Ramsey," she scoffed, again put off by his autocratic attitude. "You cannot lay claim to a baby as if he were a piece of property." She knew she was being disrespectful to the firm's biggest client, but she didn't care. Bobber deserved better.

Slender teardrops slipped out of Agatha's eyes, magnified behind her thick lenses. "I cannot believe it. After all these years. I just cannot." With a cry she collapsed on the file-strewn cushions.

"Agatha!" Caron rushed to her side, dropping down to the sofa to steady her while Ramsey reached for the telephone. With a huge, shaky finger he punched in the number of his physician's office.

"I must speak to Doctor Norwood this instant, young lady!" he was roaring into the telephone after apparently being brushed off. "I don't care if he's conferring with Doctor Spock, Doctor Kildare, or Doctor Dolittle! Yes, I do realize he's busy. I've known him forty years and pay for a chunk of that fancy suite your bottom is perched in. You tell him Douglas Ramsey is on the line. Never mind how it's spelled!"

Caron pressed her fingers against Agatha's wrist to find her pulse steady and strong. "Has she eaten anything lately?" she asked anxiously.

Ramsey shook his head. "Should've stopped, I suppose. It's my—" He broke off to turn his attention back to the telephone. "Agatha's collapsed, Fred. No, we're just around the corner at the lawyers. Right. Fifth floor, Caron Carlisle's office." He slammed down the phone. "He's coming to us."

Caron nodded in relief. "Summon my secretary, tell her to get some water in here."

Ramsey balked for a brief, surprised moment.

"Hurry up," Caron prodded, massaging Agatha's wrists.

"Yes, yes," he relented, swinging open the door and bellowing for water.

By the time the doctor arrived, Agatha was coming around. She blinked several times, struggling to take in her surroundings. Caron's heart lurched in compassion at the sight of the normally spritely woman in a vulnerable, woozy condition.

"There now, old girl," Fred Norwood said cheerily, patting Agatha's shallow cheek. The dapper man with a head of thick white hair and bright gray eyes was amazingly calm and pleasant considering the summons he'd received. "Shame on you for giving Douglas such a scare."

Agatha smiled wanly. "Where am I, Doctor?"

"Why at your attorney's, m'dear. Cutting your crabby brother out of the will, I hope." He tucked his stethoscope back into his black bag and rose from the sofa. Though nearly Ramsey's age, he was about half his size. This didn't stop him from standing up to the billionaire in doleful disgust. "This delicate flower needs constant care, fool," he chastised under his breath.

"I know it," Douglas Ramsey grumbled, stroking his chin nervously. "She all right?"

"Yes, for a frail, elderly woman who's obviously been traumatized, she's tip-top."

Ramsey rubbed the back of his neck. "She had it in her head to be here today. The baby search means so much to her. I take the blame, however. Sometimes I forget just how old the spunky gal is."

"Get her something to eat," the doctor advised. "And get her home."

"Not yet," Agatha protested feebly, struggling to sit up.

"We'll take good care of her, Doctor," Caron promised. "We've sent for some hot sandwiches and cold drinks."

"Thank you for coming, Fred," he said, seeing him to the door.

"Stop by my office soon, Douglas," the doctor directed.

"I'm in perfect health," Ramsey protested in surprise.

"You certainly are," Fred Norwood retorted, jerking open the door. "Fit enough to give my receptionist a well-deserved apology."

"Oh, give her a raise instead," he blustered in dismissal.

"Money doesn't buy everything," the doctor chided. "Maybe this baby grandson you're so intent on finding will teach you some compassion. Heaven knows none of us have had any luck."

Ramsey tried to shoot off a proper response, but his old friend was off with an airy wave.

Caron could feel Ramsey's eyes upon her as they sat around her desk a short while later, eating their take-out food. To her relief, he had the sensitivity not to probe about the photograph. Still trying to recover from her fainting spell, Agatha was eating in slow, labored bites, sipping on soda pop from one of Caron's ceramic mugs.

"Feeling better, Agatha?" Ramsey inquired gently.

"Much," she replied with a bit of her old spark.

"Excellent. Franklin will take you home then."

Agatha eyed him in sharp suspicion. "What are you planning to do in the meantime?"

"Caron is going to take me to the Wyatt boy's Laundromat. He's had my baby all this time! And he was close to James, just as I figured," he reasoned in a growl. "I knew something was burning in that man's gut the night of the party."

"Yes, but you don't understand the cir—"

"Just hold on right there," he ordered Caron sternly.

Caron clamped her mouth shut, the recipient of his wrath for the first time. Their relationship had been so congenial until now.

"I wish to be a part of this confrontation at the laundry place," Agatha insisted.

"That is impossible." He reached across the desk and gave her frail hand a squeeze. "I'm no fool, Agatha. I've got the picture now—no pun intended. That baby has your red hair, the roundness of your youth. It's enough for me, coupled with Wyatt's probing investigation at the house." Agatha tried to speak, but he held up a meaty hand. "I didn't tell you about our clash the night of the party, I know. Actually, it makes your identification all the more spontaneous, doesn't it?"

"Yes, Douglas." She threw up her hands in abdication.

"Come along then," he said, helping her to her feet. "Franklin is right outside. You two may as well start off now."

"Very well," she agreed with surprising meekness.

"Knew all along, didn't you?" Ramsey chastised as Caron pulled her Saturn out of the downtown parking lot fifteen minutes later.

Despite the intensity of the situation, Caron had to suppress a nervous giggle at the sight of the hulky billionaire stuffed into the passenger seat of her car, fingers gripped to the dashboard. She wondered how long it had been since he'd been in a regular-size vehicle.

"I don't know anything for sure, sir," she replied honestly, braking for a yellow light. "I can only say that Rick had some sort of agreement with your son, James. He asked for my assistance and I couldn't refuse."

"Some good-humor man, this Richard Wyatt," he snorted in bitterness. "In cahoots with James. With you. I don't know him from Adam and he's manipulating me like a puppet on a string."

"You didn't exactly fall prey to his game, though, did you?" she pointed out.

"I offer a million dollars for information leading to my grandson and this guy harbors the child and penetrates my defenses for a closer look—through my trusted attorney!"

Caron was glad the light turned green and she could concentrate on driving the car.

"He have the medal?" he barked.

"I haven't seen it," Caron replied. "And Rick has never admitted that the baby is the right one. Not yet, he hasn't."

"Why not?" he asked in surprise.

"I don't think he wanted to put me in that tight of a spot," she explained in Rick's defense. "I believe he was trying to keep me in the dark for my own good. So I wouldn't feel obligated to turn Bobber in."

"So, he believes you do have a shred of loyalty toward your client," Ramsey snapped sarcastically.

"Believe it or not, I have been looking out for your interests, too, sir," she assured him. "You wouldn't be happy if the baby wasn't where he really belonged. Rick just wanted to make sure of where that was."

"What did he promise you?" Ramsey wondered incredulously. "Fortune?"

"Love," Caron replied just above a whisper, keeping her eyes on the road. "Rick and I do go a long way back, Mr.

Ramsey. He came to me because of our link, for help in honoring your son's last request."

"What request?"

"He wished for Rick to decide upon the fate of your grandchild."

"The arrogance!" Ramsey exploded in rage. "He's nothing more than a—a—"

"Rebel?"

"Exactly!"

"Last requests are important, sir," Caron reasoned. "Rick was closer to James than he let on and took his death extremely hard. He's been riding on emotion ever since. I believe fulfilling James's last wish is part of his grieving process. He desperately wants to do the right thing for the heir. Without jeopardizing my job, by the way."

"Foolish girl!" he muttered in disbelief. "I could have your job with the snap of a finger."

"I know," Caron agreed. "But I'd do it again. For Rick. For James. Please try to see this as a happy ending to your quest, sir," she pleaded. "Rick assured me the child's mother was due back today."

Ramsey's face beamed in satisfaction. "Ah, now we're getting somewhere."

11

"WHY, THE PLACE IS buttoned up tight. In the middle of the afternoon!"

Caron was expressing her surprise to Douglas Ramsey as they stood on the sidewalk outside Hotshots a short time later, staring at the Closed sign in the shuttered window-pane. Her heart pounded in her ears as she imagined the worst. What if Rick flew the coop with the baby, leaving her with the consequences?

"Maybe he's inside." Caron moved toward the door, trying to keep up a calm front.

"He's probably harboring the baby's mother in there," Ramsey theorized in anger. Edging past her, he raised a large fist to the door. "C'mon, c'mon," he bellowed. "Open up I say!"

Miraculously, a rattle soon signified that someone was working the locks from the inside.

Rick swung the door open wide, drilling the man with a penetrating look. "Open up or what, sir? You going to blow my house in?"

"I just might!"

Rick stepped into the doorway, completely filling it with his wide, solid form. He easily kept them at bay by bracing his powerful arms on either side of the wooden jamb.

Caron watched him metamorphose into the Hotshot with three simple actions: the lift of his square chin, the slit of his eyelids, the slouch of the left shoulder. An inherent warrior stance, honed to perfection by years and years of rebellion. To an authority figure like Douglas Ramsey, the act was utter arrogance, calculated defiance. But Caron could read the real story behind the shield these days. Rick was arming himself against an internal attack more than anything else, determined not to give in to his own frailties.

"The time has come, Rick," she said in soft counterpoint.

Rick looked at her for a long, stubborn moment. What was he waiting for? she wondered, gazing into the depths of his troubled eyes. Ramsey had the goods on him and that was that. "Rick, you really have nothing more to lose at this point," she stated quietly.

"I hope you're right." With a resigned sigh, he stepped aside, allowing them to enter.

"I know everything, young man," Ramsey charged impatiently.

"I doubt it," Rick retorted. "But do come in. I prefer to clean all dirty linen behind closed doors around here."

Rick fiddled with the blinds as they stepped inside, allowing daylight to flood the place. He did keep the Closed sign in place, however.

Caron scanned the place to find one surprising visitor on hand in the stuffy silence. Agatha, alert and rejuvenated, was seated in one of the red vinyl chairs beside the pop machine.

"What are you doing here, Agatha?" Ramsey demanded in amazement. "The doctor said—"

"Never mind what Fred said to do," she cut in, her voice and eyes bright. "I'm back in form. As good as it gets these days, anyway."

"Where is the limousine? Where is Franklin?" Douglas Ramsey blustered.

"I sent him for a luncheon break," Agatha replied saucily. "He won't be back for an hour."

"Why, I'll have his head!"

"You most certainly will not," she chided. "I was bound to get here one way or the other. Franklin's wise enough to know when he's licked. Which is more than I can say for you!"

"But why are you here, m'dear?" he asked in a softer tone of total bewilderment.

Agatha's catlike eyes gleamed. "Because I have some answers and want more."

"I know it all now," Ramsey informed her. "Caron has filled me in on this man's connection to James, to the baby in the picture. Wyatt here will not deny us our heir any longer. If he tries, I shall have him up on charges."

"Now, Mr. Ramsey," Caron swiftly interceded, "surely we can calmly sort this thing out." To her frustration, Caron realized that Ramsey wasn't paying the least bit of attention to her, but looking at something over her shoulder. She whirled to find Rick's sister emerging from the storage room with Bobber in her arms. "Erin?" she ventured in surprise.

"Yes. Hello, Caron." Erin punctuated her greeting with a sunny smile as she tossed a curtain of blond hair out of Bobber's reach. "It's been a long time."

"Years," Caron clarified, taking in the younger woman's tanned skin and slender form set to advantage in a springy floral dress. "You look wonderful, as if you've just stepped off the beach."

"Well, you're close," Erin admitted. "My husband, Ben, and I just got back from Mexico."

"I would like to hold the boy if I may," Ramsey requested in brusque impatience.

Erin shot her big brother a questioning glance.

Rick nodded solemnly, his black lashes fanning his sharp cheekbones. "Let him hold the baby. He won't drop him."

Bobber went willingly to Ramsey, inquisitively fingering the golden clip clasping his maroon tie to his snowy white shirt. "You'll be wearing one of those on your ties some day," Ramsey told him in singsong pleasure.

"So, Mr. Ramsey, just what about Bobber tipped you off?" Rick asked with new suspect civility in his tone.

"Nothing!" Ramsey replied bluntly. "I imagine Agatha has explained about the photographs of your mountain trip. Her memory was jogged, not mine. Imagine the nerve of this upstart thinking he'll decide if I'm fit to be your grandpapa!" he told Bobber, bouncing him in his arms.

"Douglas," Agatha warned.

"Ah, what?" he asked, tearing his eyes from the child.

"Don't you wonder just how I identified the heir?"

"The red hair, round face, I see it all now. Don't worry, Agatha. If you're on hand to pave the way, you have nothing to fret about. If the medal isn't here, we'll just have to wait for the blood tests for positive proof."

Agatha opened her curled hand to reveal the silver dollar medallion on its original chain.

Ramsey moved forth with Bobber to get a closer look. "By George, it's the one!" He looked over at Rick in accusation. "So you did have it all along."

"James gave it to me, along with his note asking for help," Rick explained.

"Douglas, there is something I wish to explain," Agatha again tried to intercede."

"What? That Rick Wyatt deserves the reward for finding the heir?"

"Rick does deserve the reward," Agatha agreed with a cagey grin.

"So be it," Ramsey conceded. "I have what I want."

Agatha's lined face narrowed in disgust. "You don't even know what you have!"

"Of course I do. I have James's baby in my arms. What I don't have, however, is the mother. She will have to be dealt with. And Caron promised me she'd be here today."

"Calm down and listen to me," Agatha directed with unexpected force. "The heir is the spittin' image of James's first love. Her name is Julia. I spotted the resemblance immediately. It's truly uncanny."

Ramsey's head spun in all directions. "How can she be his first? Where is this woman? I wish to speak to her right now."

"She doesn't wish to mix with any of us, Douglas."

"You are talking utter nonsense, woman. You haven't fully recovered from your fainting episode."

Caron blinked in shock. Was Agatha confused? As confused as Caron was herself?

Erin made the next move, stepping up to take Bobber from Ramsey's arms. Caron watched as the infant curled into Erin, content as a babe in his mother's arms. And why not? she slowly speculated, as the pair joyously engaged in a flurry of tickles and giggles.

The baby was in his mother's arms.

Erin was Bobber's mother!

And she had appeared on schedule, just as Rick had predicted. Just as Rick had known she would—probably well in advance. Bobber's father was no doubt Erin's husband Ben, a former classmate of theirs. Ben with the bright red hair.

This led to one certain deduction: Bobber was not the Ramsey heir. Caron's analytical brain ticked crazily over the puzzle pieces, sorting them, fitting them into one larger picture. The entire thing reeked of a setup.

As for the mysterious Julia, old flame to James, she had to be a little too old to bear anyone's child. And she wanted nothing to do with the Ramseys, according to Agatha.

One long look into Agatha's clear eyes convinced Caron that the woman knew exactly what she was saying.

With that decision made, she shifted her gaze to Rick. Their eyes locked for a long, startling moment. And the answer to the riddle was finally clear.

"I never said Bobber was the one," he reminded her.

Caron felt her hackles rise as she thought back on all the trust she'd offered him. All the detours he'd taken from the simple truth. "Quit beating around the bush, Rick. I deserve to hear it all from you."

"The Bobber is my nephew," Rick confessed. "I've been caring for him while Erin and her husband took a well-deserved vacation."

"Don't be so modest, Rick," Erin urged, turning to Caron. "The trip was his idea. He even helped with the arrangements."

"And insisted upon caring for the Bobber," Caron deduced.

Erin nodded with a laugh. "I wish you'd all stop calling my baby by that ridiculous nickname. Rick made it up for him because his round head resembles a fishing bobber, red on top and white on the bottom. His real name is Ricky, after his generous uncle."

"Wily is right!" Caron seethed between her teeth.

"I want my heir, dammit," Ramsey bellowed. "Everyone is talking riddles."

"There's your heir, sir," Caron proclaimed with bitter force, in a grand sweeping gesture toward Rick. "Agatha claims to have recognized him in the photograph, and I know it's not me."

"But, but—" Ramsey gaped in befuddlement. "James told Agatha he had a baby. You are a grown man, Richard."

"Many parents regard their children in those terms," Rick pointed out. "Especially at sentimental moments. He knew his life was draining away when he confided in Agatha."

"Don't you faint on me now," Agatha cautioned her brother moments later as Caron and Rick eased him into a chair beside her.

"This is preposterous," Ramsey mumbled, looking lost for the first time in Caron's memory. "I am so confused."

"It's simple really," Rick ventured to explain. "I am your grandson, sir. I've known so for a few years now. James simply walked in here one day to announce that he was my natural father. I've known my whole life that I'm an adopted child, as are Erin and my two other siblings. Our brood is a patchwork of genes, but it hasn't stopped us from being a tight-knit family."

"Why'd he wait so long to claim you?" Ramsey asked. "And he thought I was a neglectful father...."

Rick jumped to his natural father's defense with lightning speed. "James had just learned that he'd fathered a child. My natural mother had an attack of conscience when she heard his health was failing and contacted him. He immediately investigated and tracked me down."

"Oh, I see," Ramsey mumbled, removing his glasses to rub his eyes. "It seems I've missed the real facts all along by jumping to conclusions."

Rick took pleasure in affirming it. "James was heartsick over the years we lost. But we made the most of our time together by nurturing a close friendship." He paused to get a grip on his emotions. "He wasn't sure I should ever take the risk of contacting you, fearful that you'd intrude on my happiness. But, in the end, he ultimately felt I should have the option. All he asked, was that I wait until after his passing. I wasn't sure we could make a go of it, so I brought the Bobber in as a decoy and contacted Caron." He cast her a look of apology, yearning for a glimmer of understanding, of forgiveness in her eyes. But only the pain of his betrayal reflected back at him, shooting daggers into his heart. "Caron didn't want to deceive you," he assured Ramsey, unable to face her any longer. "I persuaded her, tricked her."

"I had more faith in your abilities as an attorney," Ramsey chastised her in disappointment.

"I am still a good attorney!" she hastened to interject. "Just a foolish lover."

Rick's gaze tore to her again, his muscled body frozen in anguish. He couldn't argue such a personal issue in front of these people. He wanted nothing more than to throw her over his shoulder and run for the hills. Force the empty look out of her eyes with ardent lovemaking and passionate promises. But he owed the Ramseys something, after the hullabaloo he'd caused.

"I didn't mean anyone any harm, sir," he assured. "I thought I was clever enough to check you out without any fuss. But what did we do but end up in an instant flare-up. I walked away the night of your party with no intention of ever seeing you again. But you were clever enough to see there was more to my story than met the eye. Inherent stubbornness and determination kept us in the same arena."

"So you thought you'd put off the inevitable by whisking me off to the mountains!" Caron lashed out. "Hide out as long as you could!"

"For Pete's sake, Caron, we were only gone one night!" he reasoned.

"But it was enough to get me where you wanted me."

"Yes, in a marrying mood!" he admitted, causing the Ramseys to gasp. "Sorry, folks. But I'm not going to let this woman get away a second time." He whirled back to her. "Caron, I knew the charade was crumbling and I wanted to solidify our relationship beforehand. I love you, honey," he declared passionately. "You have to believe that."

"I can't believe any of this!" she wailed, all professional poise thrown to the wind, despite the importance of the client on hand. "How silly I must've looked, hot on the trail of the red-hair link between Agatha and the baby."

"The red hair turned out to be a welcome red herring," Rick conceded, biting back a twitching smile. "It's just an accident that Erin's husband is a carrot top."

"None of this erases your part in this deception, Miss Carlisle," Ramsey chastised. "You should've reported Rick's scheme to me immediately."

"Yes, sir," Caron readily agreed, twisting the handles of her purse in trembling fingers. "It would have simplified things for all of us."

"She had the heir's best interest in mind," Rick broke in forcefully. "Even though she didn't know I was the heir in question. And it was the way James wanted it, too!"

"I expect utter loyalty from anyone in my employ," Ramsey insisted, lowering his fist to the arm of his chair.

"Oh, hush up, you big bully," Agatha scoffed. "Carrie did the best she could. She will always be my good friend. And yours too."

"I believe this is a good time for me to leave," Caron said with a shaky sigh. "I'm expected back at work."

"I can't lose you again, Caron," Rick pleaded. He knew the moment she walked out the door, the spell between them would be broken. If he could make her understand now while the wound was fresh. It would swiftly heal.

Caron's face crumpled in anguish. "Total trust you said! And I believed you!"

"I was trying to shield you!"

"You used me."

"I never thought it would go this far." Rick stared at her bleakly. "Please believe that I'm out of secrets."

"I'm out of faith, Rick," she choked out. She blinked several times in an effort to check the tears in her eyes, hoping she wouldn't break down in public.

"Please don't be upset, Carrie," Agatha chirped beseechingly.

"Don't go, Caron," Rick pleaded, grabbing for her arm.

"You've already made me look like a total incompetent in front of these clients," she snapped in his ear. "Let me leave with the last shred of dignity I possess."

Rick dropped his hand from her arm, unable to argue her point. With a final apology to the Ramseys, she made her exit.

"Well, at least everything is out in the open now," Agatha murmured, looking up to Rick with loving, misty eyes. "I, for one, am delighted that our heir is long out of diapers. We can begin to build a memorable relationship right away. Right, Douglas?"

"I was expecting a bouncy baby who wouldn't talk back," Ramsey grumbled. "Who'd offer a little unconditional love to a poor old man."

"You would try to force a miracle," Rick grumbled, eyes darting to the window as Caron's Saturn rolled off down the street. "Unconditional love doesn't exist, man. You can't even buy it with all your dough."

"How can you say such things?" Agatha scoffed. "You of all people, Rick Wyatt, know that Carrie's love for you has been unconditional. And as for miracles—" her sparkling eyes wandered to her brother "—you've brought this crusty old dog a second chance. A red-herring stunt second only to the parting of the Red Sea."

Rick drove his hands through his hair with a mighty groan. He'd lost the best thing that had ever happened to him for a second time. Hoping James would forgive his flare of regret, he fervently wished with all his heart that he'd left well enough alone with the Ramseys. He shouldn't have needed such a monumental excuse to contact Caron in the first place. He should've called her last week in honor of the new Chinese place opening down the street.

"GIVE ME THOSE CUPCAKES this instant, Caron!" Megan ordered, chasing Caron around their kitchen table. The nurse had awakened around dinnertime the same day to find her roommate wolfing down bakery cakes smothered in rich chocolate frosting.

"Let me eat myself into oblivion," Caron cried with a full mouth, dodging the small blonde in the striped jammies.

"I can't. Nurses are dedicated to saving lives." With a grunt, she jerked the box from Caron's hands. "Now," she said, her eyes narrowing in professional interrogation, "just how many of these have you taken in the last hour?"

Caron glared at her, a huge chocolate ring around her belligerently set mouth. "Not enough to numb the pain."

"Oh, you've had enough, all right," Megan deduced as she counted the frosting smudges in the box.

"If you don't give me those back, I'll just get them somewhere else," Caron threatened with a shaking fist.

"Let's just calm down," Megan placated, pulling out two chairs at the table.

"I don't want to," Caron said with a defiant lift to her chin.

"Sit!" Megan ordered, shoving her into a chair.

Already limp from the events of the day, Caron sank down at the table like a rag doll, resting her head in her arms. Megan set the box on the counter and sat down beside her. "Now, we're dealing with something big," she calculated. "Really, really big."

Caron nodded from the shelter of her arms.

"Your mother flipped out at the Laundromat," Megan guessed. "She found out about your second stained dress and—" She abruptly stopped in midtheory as the back of Caron's brown head rocked back and forth.

"It's Rick," she croaked hollowly.

"Rick broke up with you," Megan proposed, only to receive another negative head rock. "No? Then Ramsey found out that Rick's harboring his fugitive grandson. Bingo!" She snapped her fingers. "The whole thing came tumbling down around your ears."

"Yes."

"Bobber is now the happy recipient of a cool billion," Megan murmured, shaking her head in wonder.

"No."

"Yes, no," Megan squawked in frustration. "Where have I gone wrong?"

"Rick is the billionaire baby!" she told her in a muffle.

"Come again!" Megan shrieked, pulling Caron up in her seat.

Caron nodded numbly, fresh tears springing to her eyes. "It's true, Meggy. He was the real heir all along. Bobber is his sister Erin's boy. He used him as a decoy and me as a go-between chump. Wanted to see if the Ramsey scene was for him before committing himself."

"He borrowed the baby to throw the scent off his trail while he mingled in the thick of things?"

"Exactly."

Megan gaped. "Gee, the guy's pretty smart."

"Too smart for the likes of me," Caron said languishingly. "I fell for his charms again. At my age!"

Megan reached across the table to squeeze her hand. "I thought he loved you."

"He says he does, but who can believe him after the stunt he's pulled?"

"Couldn't you try?" Megan coaxed.

Caron pursed her mouth stubbornly. "I can't think of one reason."

Megan balked. "I can think of a billion of 'em."

"Megan, the man, not the money, is at issue here."

"Your mother would be ashamed of such talk," Megan teased. "But you are right, of course. Shall I go and defend your honor?" she suggested fiendishly. "Pummel that bad boy's chest in your name?"

"Thanks for the offer, but I think it will be best to put Rick behind us for good."

Megan lowered her small fist on the table with determination. "Consider him completely forgotten."

Caron nodded numbly with a sniff. "Right after you fulfill the bet, he'll be history."

Megan's face fell. "Rats. Thought I had ya there."

12

"YOU ARE THIRTY MINUTES late!" Rick whirled on Kyle in fury as he entered Hotshots Friday afternoon. "I can't go out to lunch with you anymore. Ma has to leave. She has a dental appointment."

"Ah, Rick, it can't be that late." Kyle slowly sauntered inside. Dressed in a conservative dark suit, with an open bag of potato chips in his hand and a mischievous grin on his face, he was a mass of contradictions in himself. He followed Rick's jabbing finger up at the large round school clock on the wall. "Gee, I did lose track of time," he yielded in genuine surprise. "I've got to get back to the office myself pretty soon."

Rick glared at him. "Where the hell have you been?"

Kyle's face glowed. "It was the craziest thing, Rick. I was passing by Marshall's Market next door. Around noon, right on schedule," he hastened to add in his own defense.

"You trip outside and hit your head on the curb?" Rick asked, his black brows arching in menace.

"Whew, aren't you the touchy billionaire baby today," Kyle grumbled. "They say all really rich people are miserable inside. Must be true."

"Only poor people say so," Rick snorted. "And I'm not sittin' on a billion, not yet."

"It's only a matter of time, really, until you and Grandpa Ramsey come to terms—of endearment." Kyle sank into one of the red vinyl chairs against the wall, dipping a long-fingered hand into his bag of potato chips. "In the meantime, you have a million to tide you over."

"I deserved the reward money. Led the old man right to the heir, just as he wanted." Rick leaned over Kyle, resting his hands on the chrome armrests of his chair. "Tell me why, Kyle," he invited in false cheeriness. "Tell me why I asked Ma to cover for me during the lunch hour, only to have you waste her time and mine."

"Where is Ma?" Kyle wondered, sand-colored hair falling into his eyes as he anxiously scanned the room. "Ma?" he called out.

"She won't protect you this time," Rick warned, his hands locking Kyle's wrists to the chrome arms of the chair, nearly crushing his chip bag.

"She likes to, makes her feel young. Ma!" he hollered.

Eleanor emerged from the back room with an armload of mini detergent boxes. "Oh, hello, Kyle. Finally got here, did you?"

"I was just going to tell Rick about my dream girl, Ma. Thought you might want to hear about it."

"I'm all ears," Eleanor said brightly, scooting up the aisle. "Ricky's certainly interested," she noted, beaming over the brotherly scene. "Hunched over you like an eager cat."

"Yeah, right." Kyle gulped down the chips in his mouth, smiling under his brother's glare. "Anyway, I was passing by the market, and I noticed the place was stuffed with people. A cheering throng. I got to figuring they must be giving something away in there."

"So are they, Kyle?" Eleanor dumped the detergent boxes on a washing machine in preparation for a hasty exit.

"Slow down, Ma. It wasn't anything like that at all. Megan Gage was roller-skating through the aisles of the store, dressed in her old gym suit, singing our old high school fight song.

"'Cheer, cheer for Truman High,'" he sang out, catching Rick by the arm before he could bolt off. "Slow down, brother," he advised under his breath. "They're not giving any of that away, either. Caron was the first to leave the scene."

"Why didn't you come get me, brother?" Rick demanded. The fact that she'd been in his territory for the last half hour was more than he could bear. No matter how he'd tried during the last few days to trap her for a second round, she'd managed to evade him. The firm had given her the week off as a reward for solving the billionaire heir mystery. She used the time to scatter herself to the winds.

Oh, the satisfaction she must've felt hanging around right under his nose.... Rick's fists opened and closed reflexively, as desire and desperation surged through his system.

"I was literally trapped inside the store," Kyle was telling him in genuine sympathy, greedily digging in the bag for chips now that his hands were again free of Rick's vise-grip. "You know how uncertain mob behavior can be. We were packed in there like sardines and old Pop Marshall was trying to transform spectators into customers. Can't blame him, I suppose, considering that the stunt was costing him plenty. You see, Megan may have been a roller queen at one time, but her balance isn't very good anymore. Rammed into a display of canned corn and toppled into a freezer full of frozen dinners. Cans rolled and crushed boxes flew, boy."

"Why would a grown woman do such a thing?" Eleanor clucked in astonishment.

Kyle tipped his head with a pensive sigh. "It's not for us to reason why. In those short shorts, keep a rollin' by."

Eleanor shot her elder son a sour look that he blithely ignored. "It's hard to believe that levelheaded Caron would associate with a flake like her," she mused in disapproval.

"Megan has not lost her marbles," Rick announced with great reluctance. "She did it on account of me, I'm sure." The news drew the same sort of moans and groans his rebel antics of old used to.

"You haven't stirred up this kind of fuss since high school," Eleanor clucked in confusion.

"Well, it is leftover high school stuff, really," he explained, with a dismissing wave. "She was fulfilling the terms of a bet she and Caron made years ago. The first one to get a phone call from me was the winner. The loser . . ." He paused, rolling his eyes to the ceiling. "The loser obviously had to skate through Marshall's Market on skates in her gym suit singing the school fight song."

"I imagine at the time it seemed like a frivolous debt, but now with the passing of years, I suppose it was an excruciating experience," Kyle wagered with a hearty chuckle.

Rick nodded in new empathy. "It sure explains why she's been so annoyed with me since my initial call to Caron concerning Ramsey."

"And explains the messages written on her white sweatshirt," Kyle added in further deduction. "The front said, Hotshot Is A Billionaire Bum. The back said, A Cruise Can't Cost That Much. I just figured she was speaking for Caron, so I wasn't going to tell you."

"I think each of them took her best shot at this Hot-shot," Rick wagered with a mournful shake of his head.

"You still know how to get the girls goin'," Kyle marveled, drawing a frown from Rick.

"Hadn't you better get back to your job, Kyle?" Eleanor pointed out.

"Well, I wouldn't have to worry about it if I were a bil-lionaire," Kyle grumbled, extending his long legs in the aisle as if no longer in such a hurry. "Say, maybe my blood kin has a wad, too," he pondered in sudden inspiration.

"A wad of something," Rick gibed, knowing full well that Kyle, like many adoptees, had no interest in search-ing for his natural parents.

"So, now all of a sudden being a Wyatt isn't good enough for my boys," Eleanor scolded with an edge of panic.

"Oh, c'mon, Ma," Rick scoffed, his tone softening with his features. "I've told you a hundred times since James popped into my life, that you and Pa are the only folks I want."

"Yes," she agreed with a sniff. "James made it easy for all of us by accepting you on your terms—moving into the neighborhood, nurturing a friendship with no strings at-tached. But his father wants so much more. He wants you heart and soul."

"He's an old man looking for a second chance," Rick relented quietly. "I've had more patience for his position since accepting that." Rick had done a lot of thinking during the past few days. As he longed for mercy from Caron for the underhanded stunt he'd pulled, the more mercy he offered to the billionaire in search of absolu-tion. "I stopped by his barn of a house last night. We talked. Hell, we argued!" he corrected. "We both have a history of being a bit difficult, but I think we can come to some sort of a truce, maybe even some common ground. For instance, we both agree that Caron's role in my deception should be kept from the law firm. But we fought over who treated her with more understanding. The old goat really has a soft spot for her underneath it all!"

"And you know I was only teasing you, Ma," Kyle chimed in, laboriously rising to his feet with his crumpled bag of chips to envelop Eleanor in a bear hug. "We've always been rich in our own way."

"Certainly what I've taught you!" she huffed with a shadow of a smile. "No one would put up with you boys, anyway, not the way I do."

"Could you do me a favor?" Kyle asked, cupping her face in his hands.

"I'll try," she ventured, brushing some salt from his chin.

"Tell Ricky to fix me up with Megan, will ya, huh?"

"Are you sure she's your type?" Eleanor wondered dubiously.

"She's a nurse," Kyle promptly reported, bringing a shine of approval to his mother's face.

"You work something out, Ricky," Eleanor directed. "Arrange something nice for your brother and this roller skater."

"Hey, I don't even have a girl anymore," Rick exploded incredulously, aiming a thumb at his expansive chest.

"Oh, yes, you do," she huffed with a sigh. "You help Kyle."

"Megan does deserve a cruise, I guess...." he mused, stroking his square chin. "Do I dare further torment her by sending you along on the same ship?"

"Sounds like the perfect setup," Kyle agreed excitedly. "Make it first class for both of us."

"Make it separate cabins for each of them," Eleanor automatically inserted. "Now, I'm afraid I must be off to my beauty parlor appointment," she said with a glance to her watch.

"I thought you were going to the dentist," Rick recalled in confusion.

Eleanor's round cheeks grew pink. "Well, I was going to surprise you, but I am really going to have my hair tinted."

"Because of what Deborah Carlisle said?" Rick demanded.

"Yes and no," Eleanor replied. "You see, Deborah can be a real pain, but she does know a lot about color and style. I have faith in her advice, no matter how rudely it happens to be delivered."

Rick growled in frustration. "She doesn't deserve a friend like you, Ma."

"She'll be back just the same," Eleanor predicted with a twinkle. "Ironically enough, she'd never let the son-in-law catch of the century get away—now that he is the catch of the century." Eleanor kissed Rick's pained face with a smack. "You must learn to laugh over the irony of Deborah's shallowness. It's hard to say that even in time, she will ever acquire any depth. I give Caron credit for accepting this and working around it."

"I really don't think we will have to concern ourselves with Caron or her mother ever again," Rick complained.

"Well, life does hold a surprise or two, does it not?" Eleanor pointed out wistfully.

Rick shook his head. "Caron thinks I betrayed her trust."

"She has a right to be angry. But in your defense, you didn't deliberately hurt her."

"Wouldn't have shamelessly used her, if you'd known it would destroy her," Kyle helpfully appended.

"How was I to know I'd fall apart at the mere sight of her after all these years?" Rick challenged to no one in particular. "That we were both an amorous accident just waiting to collide? I tried to back off, but she wouldn't let me. We just tumbled deeper and deeper into ourselves, into this missing heir thing. I thought I had control, but I never did, not really."

He paused with a resigned sigh, closing his eyes to find Caron there. He shook the vision away, just as he'd done a thousand times during the past few days. "Maybe I just don't deserve her."

"Let her be the judge, Ricky," Eleanor advised. "It will be good for your rebel soul to show a little humility this once."

"Yeah," Kyle added, rubbing his hands together in greedy anticipation. "Having the chance to kick you around after all these years should give her a little satisfaction."

Rick's annoyance with Kyle uncorked in a burst of laughter. "Shut up, big brother, or I'll book you on a budget cruise—aboard *Jaws*."

Kyle pointed at his mother as she prepared to speak. "Don't say it, Ma. Don't tell him separate sharks."

"PINCH ME AND TELL ME it's real."

"Pinch you, Caron?" Megan turned away from the ticket counter at Stapleton International Airport, a validated pass in her hand. "I'm the one going on the cruise."

It was an overcast day in late November, shortly after dawn. Megan was decked out in a royal blue outfit fit for

Princess Diana. Caron looked like little more than a peddler in her faded jeans and worn fringed suede jacket.

"I know you're going on the trip," Caron agreed with a smirk. "But as you wing off to connect with your ship in Miami, I'll be zipping back to the town house for a nice long breakfast before work. Bound and determined to make all sorts of noises I can't make while you're sleeping."

"What a clown!" Megan hooted. Then, tipping her curly blond head in afterthought she added, "After that roller-skating fiasco a few weeks ago, maybe I should be the one pinching you."

"It wasn't as much fun as I thought it would be," Caron wistfully confessed as they sank down into molded chairs, Megan's belongings scattered at their feet. "Winning the bet, I mean."

"I think it would've been a lot more fun for both of us ten years ago," Megan mused, patting Caron's knee in consolation.

Caron appreciated Megan's unyielding support since her breakup with Rick. She would miss her desperately during the next two weeks. She hadn't felt this alone in years.

"I guess we can't go back and heal those old adolescent wounds, can we?" Caron eventually theorized softly, thinking of how that decade-late call had changed her life so profoundly. And that of Rick's as well. He was in line to inherit a fortune! Megan's dues had been paid out in the open with a simple spin through the market, over in a matter of minutes. Caron knew she'd be working through her dues with an aching heart for a long, long time.

Megan released a meditative sigh. "No, we can't truly go back. We've grown up too much. Even if we could somehow return in a time warp, it would be through new, wiser eyes."

"I sure don't feel any smarter," Caron grumbled, shoving her hands into the pockets of her jacket. "And trying to recapture a lost passion was a stupid stunt."

"But what you had with Rick was far more than a stab at nostalgia," Megan protested.

"Maybe I don't deserve anything more than a lesson out of this," Caron philosophized. "I went after him with the express purpose of landing on top of him."

"Well, I imagine you accomplished that." Megan fluttered long, innocent lashes.

"Very funny," Caron retorted, unamused by the earthy pun.

"Well, I personally have a very soft spot for Rick these days," Megan airily admitted. "After all, he did come through with this trip."

"Yes, a prince of a rebel," Caron snapped tartly. She was perplexed by his good deed. She'd spent the days after their blowup convincing herself he was still nothing more than a wolf, preying on the female population for his own amusement. Then he'd come across with this surprise for Megan. . . .

"Wipe that suspicious scowl off your face," Megan chided. "He said he felt remorseful over the leftover bet, and my subsequent humiliating roller ride."

"If he's such a generous benefactor, where is my trip?" Caron demanded. "I'm the one he drew into the thick of his crazy scheme. The one he drew undercover. I nearly lost my job over this! If Mr. Ramsey hadn't kept quiet about my part in things, the partners would've had me for lunch."

"Concrete proof that there must be a merciful streak in the Ramsey clan," Megan maintained.

Caron rolled her eyes. "Oh, sure."

"Maybe Rick has different plans for you," Megan blurted out, bringing a cloud to her friend's face. "I mean, maybe he's going to pay you back some other way."

The boarding call for first-class passengers crackled over the speakers as they each silently mulled the thought.

"Well, this is it, kid." Caron stood up with her antsy friend, giving Megan a fierce hug.

"Take care, Caron." Megan gathered together her baggage and with a final peck to Caron's cheek, joined the passengers streaming into the boarding area.

Caron waited until Megan disappeared out of sight, then with a glance at her watch, moved out of the gate area into the crowded terminal corridor.

"You look absolutely naked without a baby in your arms."

Caron halted at the sound of the rich voice in her ear, spinning around to collide with chocolate eyes and a mile-wide chest.

"You!" she lashed out, instantly breaking the promise she'd made to herself to handle their next encounter coolly. But she couldn't help herself. This rebel always managed to catch her heart off guard. Always had the edge, the power to reduce her to a fragile schoolgirl. Undoubtedly she'd never outgrow his effect on her.

"You without Bobber..." He rubbed his mustache as he took full inventory of her. "You look so empty-handed somehow."

"You've described me to a T," she returned evenly, hoping to disguise the shudder rippling down her shoulders. "Empty-handed."

"You did cut your teeth on him, so to speak," he wistfully continued. "Learned everything you ever wanted to know about Bobbers, but were afraid to ask."

"Yes, I'll never forget him," she promised.

"Lucky guy."

What on earth was he doing here? she wondered.

"So, is Megan aboard the plane already?" he asked conversationally as if reading her thoughts.

"Yes. You are a funny guy, Hotshot," Caron blurted out in mystification, knowing she should avoid the lure of banter, and scamper. But she couldn't let it lie. After all she'd been through, she had to have her say one last time. "You send me over the moon with your crummy scheme, jeopardize my job—then you turn around and give Megan a vacation for roller-skating through a market. And come to see her off!" she added, obviously disbelieving the final affront the most.

Rick absorbed the verbal blow with a tilt to his chin. "Is that what you really think, Quick Draw?" he chided.

"The facts stack up only one way. Even Perry Mason would agree."

"Jealous?"

Caron reared back huffily. "Of which part?"

He was completely dominating her space despite the foot traffic around them. "I wasn't about to send you off on a romantic cruise without the Hotshot here as escort. And I couldn't get away. Besides," he added on an injured note, "you've been a hard woman to pin down, for an invitation of any kind."

Caron raised her chin, avoiding his eyes. "Well, you stopped trying."

"I'm a hothead."

"So I get no reward for all my mental anguish," she sought to confirm in surprise.

"You get me," he offered.

"What an egotistical offer, after scrambling out here to see Megan off."

Rick tipped his black head in the direction of the gate. "I'm here seeing Kyle off," he corrected.

"He's taking Megan's trip?" she asked softly, her heart alight with the news.

"Why, you didn't think I was interested in Megan—then or now, did you?" he hooted in amazement.

"Not ever!" she lied.

"I told you Kyle was the one who—"

"I know, I know," she cut in, a hot flush heating her skin.

"You just want me all for yourself," he teased.

She did.

It took all Caron's willpower not to melt into the folds of his shiny leather jacket, not to stand on tiptoe and nuzzle the morning stubble on his chin. His scent was drawing her in, making her woozy with yearning, with the need to be cuddled and reassured as only Rick could. But he couldn't just swoop back and make her swoon. He needed to prove his intentions. And it would be a tough sale after this last stunt of his.

"Yeah, Kyle's sailing the love boat," Rick replied, obviously unaware of her quivering insides. "He deserves the trip, too. He's always around when I need him." Rick winced, then laughed. "Man, will it be a nice break not to have him around when I don't need him for a change."

"Just how intimate is this dating-game prize?" she demanded with a sudden urge to play mother hen.

"Not very. They're seated on the plane together, but their cabins are separate aboard ship. You can ask Ma," he added under her narrowed look. "She made the arrangements."

"Megan barely remembers him," Caron scoffed.

"Maybe it will be to his advantage," Rick wagered in good humor. "Unlike myself, Kyle had to struggle for the girls way back when."

Caron's back stiffened under her pink sweatshirt. "Megan thinks you're quite the knight, supplying her with this trip just for the asking."

He stroked his jaw with a contemplative groan. "Handling Kyle could be a bogus price to pay. Gee, I hope she didn't think this was a completely free ride on the Hotshot here."

Caron's tight-lipped nod solemnized the occasion. "The end of innocence for Megan as well."

"Hey, don't lay her innocence on me, too—make me the ogre who toppled both class beauties. I take only responsibility for you, sweet thing."

"Always handy with the right line—when you want to be."

"Hey, I'm trying to prove that I'm a good guy," he asserted, anger flashing in his eyes. "That I've grown up with the sensitivity to understand the bet, and the embarrassment it's caused. Had I just called Megan after our date, called many others as well, I'd have been a better young man back then."

"Then I would've been skating through the market!" Caron argued ruefully, deliberately twisting the issue to buy time. Time to steady her quaking limbs. Time to grow a protective shell against his heady sensuality. Being angry with Rick didn't diminish his masculinity, or his attraction.

"Skating through there with Pop Marshall on your tail would've done you good back then," he taunted, grinning devilishly over her indignant gasp. "Would've given you a chance to laugh at yourself, see all of us as bungling kids. You were so serious, Caron. I thought we'd cured you of that, but—"

"Damn you, Rick!" she yelled, glancing around the bustling terminal. "This is no place to have a scene."

"This is the perfect place," he argued, capturing her flailing wrists in his hands. "Everyone gets emotional in airports."

"Over the departure of a loved one, maybe."

"You've flown off from me, haven't ya?" he reasoned, his deep husky voice catching slightly. He pushed her back out of the mainstream, crowding her into a wall of rental lockers.

"Rick, you used me to get what you wanted," Caron accused in open pain.

"Caron, you came at me for one big, fat, sex-charged payback. Now, was that very nice?"

"Well, it turned out pretty nice," she popped back with forced flair.

"Forget it, honey," he said in a rough little whisper. "You can barely pull off the power trip stuffed inside one of your armor suits, with your hair glued together in a crash helmet and your face painted in a glossy mask." His eyes gleamed in triumph. "I've lucked out. Got you cornered here in nothin' at all."

Her eyes widened. "I'm dressed."

He took a handful of the soft brown hair cupping her chin. "You're pretty much stripped down to the real girl here, the emotions ripe on your bare baby face."

"How dare you?" She tipped her chin high, but couldn't escape the heat of his breath on her scrubbed complexion, the spicy scent of his soap in her nostrils, the pressure of his hands on her shoulders. When he grazed her cheek with his thumb, she couldn't suppress the shudder of desire.

"See what I mean?"

"Okay, so we're physically attracted to each other," she conceded, as if pleading no contest to a charge of disorderly conduct.

"Together we are an inferno, babe," he uttered into her hair, his hands slipping into her jacket, kneading her waist through her soft sweatshirt.

"Well, it isn't enough," she argued.

"How about that I've always loved you and you're the only woman for me?" he persisted forcefully. His mouth curved in wicked glee. "How about that I have a rich grandpa?"

"Can I ever learn to trust you?" she wondered in exasperation.

"You've always trusted me, Quick Draw," he pointed out matter-of-factly. "Trusted me in the back seat of my Chevy, on top of my dryers, up in the mountains."

"Sex isn't everything!"

"That's sadly true," he relented in feigned remorse, pinching her chin as she tried to avert his gaze in a huff of disgust. "Listen, Caron, you never would've gone along with my scheme to check out Ramsey if you didn't believe in me. Deep inside you trusted my ability to make it right. Believed in my strength as a protector."

"I suppose," she begrudgingly agreed, giving in to the feeling of surrendering self-discovery.

"And I never would've let anyone blame you, hurt you," he asserted. "Your instincts about me have always been right, honey. I've always wanted only what was best for you. When I let you go the first time, it was the first totally unselfish act of my life."

"My romantic heart still wishes you would've come for me," she said in a broken little voice.

"I've come for you now," he proclaimed fiercely, obviously on the edge of losing it. "Caron, I love you so much. And after all the dodging you did for me and the Bob, it's my honor to announce that you've replaced Perry Mason as my favorite mouthpiece."

"Now there's something," she acknowledged with a sniff.

"Darn tootin' it is! Marry me, honey," he coaxed in desperation, cradling her face in his huge hands. "Just as we planned on the mountain trip. We'll have a half-dozen Bobbers. Pester your mother into behaving like a person. Air out that musty place of Ramsey's."

"But we'll fight," she protested. "We always have."

"A good debate heats the blood," he scoffed in dismissal. "Actually," he confided with a roguish slant to his mustache, "I'm sorta looking forward to it. Even to losing a skirmish once in a while on pure technicality. To the winner go the spoils, baby," he uttered huskily in her ear.

"Well, what about the Laundromat?" she persevered in doubt.

"It'll go on as always, of course," he replied in surprise.

"But Mr. Ramsey told me you're going to be dipping into his business affairs. I don't want you to change into your grandfather, Rick."

"Fat chance! Though I am going to spend some apprentice time at his headquarters, I will always be the owner and operator of Hotshots. I have plenty of family backup, more with you at my side. Why, it's a neighborhood monument!" he charged on passionately. "The place of my comeback. The place of your yellow-hatted entrance. The place we rediscovered . . . Well, face it, the old Chevy is long gone."

"Oh, Rick." She curled her arms around his neck burying her face in his jacket.

"Oh, Rick, what?" he asked in gentle persistence, his hands slipping beneath the back of her sweatshirt to the silkiness of her back. "You've always been so good with words, Quick Draw."

"You know."

A throat cleared in disgruntlement behind Rick, causing him to whirl on his heel.

"You are in my way," a stocky woman in a tan trench coat chortled.

"This is a private moment, madam," Rick asserted in curt dismissal.

"You two happen to be leaning against my locker, you rebellious young man!" she said, gesturing behind Caron. "Certainly no place to elicit a declaration from this woman."

"She has a point," he told Caron with dignity. "This is best settled at home atop the dryers."

"Yes, my darling," Caron yielded meekly. "With the Closed sign in the window, I trust."

Rick nodded firmly. "Of course. You have any pressing appointments today?"

"I'm due at jail this afternoon. What of your day?"

"The limo is picking me up later on. . . ." he trailed off loftily. "Franklin could drop you off at the prison afterward."

"Sounds perfect," Caron purred.

With a nod to the dumbfounded woman, Rick took Caron by the arm and guided her into the ever-moving mass of people in the terminal.

"I still do, you know," she murmured in his ear.

He hung an arm over her shoulders in adolescent carelessness, regarding her with the pure delight reserved for youngsters and lovers. "You do?"

Feeling like a girl out of school, Caron impetuously kissed his whisker-roughened cheek in the sea of strangers. "I've loved you long and hard, Hotshot. Yesterday and today."

He flashed her a raffish grin. "Tonight, baby, don't forget about tonight."

A Note from Leandra Logan

Writing a story based on an ancient tale was a natural process. After all, the legends of old are the foundation of the modern romance novel. They've endured in their original form because they address timeless issues. Goodness, justice, fair play, and, of course, true love. It is the adventurous quest that thrills us, the ultimate triumph over all that satisfies us. That's entertainment, with an inspiring lesson.

The tale of Rumpelstiltskin has always appealed to me because the protagonist is a female. With that in mind, I created Caron Carlisle—a problem-solving whiz who finds herself on the trail of a billion-dollar heir. What begins as little more than a riddle to her soon blossoms into a very personal affair of the heart. Caron must face the fact that she is fighting for a baby she is too frightened to handle. But struggle she does, risking her job and her heart for those old-fashioned values we all hold dear. Rest assured, she is living happily ever after with the man of her dreams.

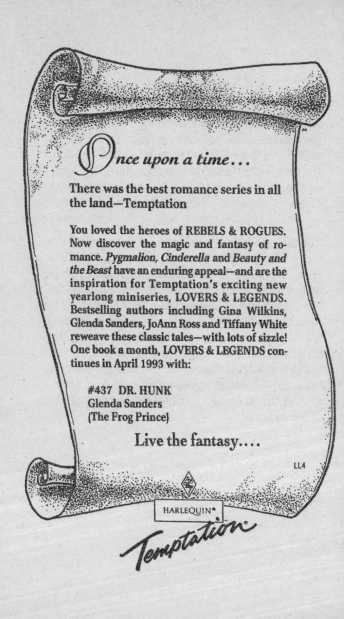

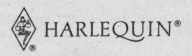

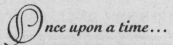

THERE WAS A FABULOUS
PROOF-OF-PURCHASE OFFER
AVAILABLE FROM

As you enjoy your Harlequin Temptation LOVERS & LEGENDS stories each and every month during 1993, you can collect four proofs of purchase to redeem a lovely opal pendant! The classic look of opals is always in style, and this necklace is a perfect complement to any outfit!

One proof of purchase can be found in the back pages of each LOVERS & LEGENDS title ... one every month during 1993!

LIVE THE FANTASY ...

To receive your gift, mail this certificate, along with four (4) proof-of-purchase coupons from any Harlequin Temptation LOVERS & LEGENDS title plus $2.50 for postage and handling (check or money order—do not send cash), payable to Harlequin Books, to: **In the U.S.**: LOVERS & LEGENDS, P.O. Box 9069, Buffalo, NY 14269-9069; **In Canada**: LOVERS & LEGENDS, P.O. Box 626, Fort Erie, Ontario L2A 5X3.
Requests must be received by January 31, 1994.
Allow 4-6 weeks after receipt of order for delivery.

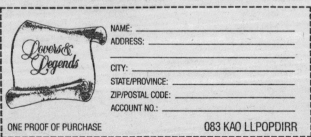

NAME: _____

ADDRESS: _____

_____

CITY: _____

STATE/PROVINCE: _____

ZIP/POSTAL CODE: _____

ACCOUNT NO.: _____

ONE PROOF OF PURCHASE

083 KAO LLPOPDIRR